Rising Storm

Kathleen Brooks

Cover art provided by Calista Taylor.
http://www.calistataylor.com

Editing provided by Karen Lawson.
http://www.theproofisinthereading.wordpress.com

Books by Kathleen Brooks

Bluegrass Series

Bluegrass State of Mind

Risky Shot

Dead Heat

Bluegrass Brothers Series

Bluegrass Undercover

Rising Storm

Secret Santa, A Bluegrass Series Novella

Acquiring Trouble

Relentless Pursuit

Secrets Collide

*For my Uncle who taught me to shoot a rifle
and told the absolute best stories.*

Prologue

K atelyn Jacks was sure she had entered the seventh ring of Hell. She would've groaned, but it hurt too much. Her head throbbed and she reached to hold it in her hands. It felt as if her brain was trying to beat its way out of her skull. The throbbing was almost unbearable and got worse when she shivered.

Why was she so cold? Her room at her grandparents' house was always warm. It was the coolness in the air that must have woken her. And why was the sun tormenting her? What had she ever done to the sun? She must've forgotten to close her blackout curtains. She thought about opening her eyes, but she was sure the sandpaper behind her eyelids would protest. What on earth had happened last night?

Katelyn buried her head into her pillow to hide from the light and think back to the night before. It was too blurry, so she went further back. It was February. She had spent the day cooking for Cade and Annie Davies' surprise party. That's right. The high school football coach and the feisty DEA agent were the ones with the surprise. The town had prepared a surprise party only to have it turn into a wedding reception that had the old guard tittering away. She had smiled at all the white and gray heads surrounding the newlyweds and playfully chastising them for getting married in secret.

It hurt, but she smiled as she blindly reached down and tried to pull the covers up. What had happened next? That's right. Sweet Trey Everett, who was a senior on the football team, had spilled his drink all down the side of her cream cashmere sweater when he realized he won the wedding pool that the Rose sisters had on the books at the café. With that money he could go to college. She had been so happy for him. She had given him a big kiss that turned him bright red. But then the fun ended.

"Hey Barbie."

"Marshall." She had replied coolly.

"How do you know when a blonde has a drinking problem?"

"You do realize I'm not some dumb blonde don't you?"

He had just smirked and ignored her, "When you wear your drinks. I gotta tell you, Barbie, I just don't get this new fashion statement you're making. I guess us dumb rednecks aren't sophisticated enough for you big New York City model types."

Marshall had spoken to her with such condescension that she had involuntarily recoiled and stepped back into the dessert table and fell against some cupcakes.

"Hmm. I guess all your model friends were right. Cupcakes go right to your ass."

"What is your problem, Marshall? What have I ever done to you?" She had been in town for over eight months and she had no clue what she had ever done to him to cause him to hate her so much.

She had had such a crush on him when she was a teenager. He was five years older than her and so cool. He had been seventeen and would ride the tractor without his shirt on. She'd hide behind the large round bales of hay in the neighboring pasture and watch as he'd bale the hay in the fields. He was always in cowboy boots, jeans, a blue University of Kentucky ball cap and nothing else.

Even she had to admit, he had aged well. His light brown hair had darkened. His hazel eyes had matured and now held lines of experience around them. His body, once lanky with youth, had filled out in ways she didn't want to admit to noticing.

"Hold on Barbie. I think I may have the answer to our problems."

She watched as he walked away and chided herself as her gaze dropped from his wide shoulders to lower on his body. He grabbed two hot cups from the refreshment table and gave sweet old Miss Lily Rose a wink before heading back to her.

"Here." He shoved the drink into her hand.

"What is this?"

"It'll help melt the icy exterior you have developed from way up there on your high horse."

"I'm not icy!"

"Whatever you say Barbie. Just drink it."

Things got fuzzy after that. She remembered talking to the newlyweds. And she remembered her friend Paige Davies, now Paige Parker, and her FBI agent husband Cole giving her a hug. She had just done a photo shoot over at Paige's store, Southern Charms, where she was modeling Paige's new hats for this year's Kentucky Derby. She remembered dancing with Paige's brother, Marshall, although she couldn't remember why she would've said yes to him after his Barbie comment. He had said it was to mend fences, but all it did was confuse her. Dancing with Marshall was an experience she was sure she'd never forget. His body rubbing against hers, his hands running down her back…

But then he had just left her on the dance floor. The Rose sisters had swooped in and started questioning her on why she was still single. The Rose sisters always reminded her of a gaggle of white-haired hens. They knew everyone and everything in town. Although they had never been married, they held firm beliefs that everyone else in town should be. There was an unspoken competition between the sisters to see who could get the most couples to marry. It didn't seem to matter she was just opening a state of the art veterinary clinic and didn't have much time to date.

That didn't stop the sisters from pointing out all the single men in the room. They started with Paul Russell, who was some sort of political son of the town. His father was a big shot in Washington D.C. and he had just won the seat as the head of the city council. He was handsome enough with his light brown hair, streaked with warm honey blonde highlights. He was about her height, maybe a half inch shorter than her and had the appearance of someone who wanted everyone to know his status in the town. Before she could think anymore of him the sisters pointed her in another direction.

She had reached down and picked up another cup of the yummy warm drink, smiled, and nodded as the sisters went on and on. Miss Lily had commented that she had made the special drinks and then she had hailed Henry Rooney over as the sisters had conveniently left.

Henry was sweet. He was the town's only defense attorney. He was handsome, but totally clueless when it came to women. She figured his law background actually hurt his game. He was so buried in his books that he didn't have the time to learn how to interact with women. He was tall, lean, but still pretty solid. His love for shiny suits got on her nerves, but his black hair was very sexy. He had asked her to dance and she remembered feeling really happy. After the dance she got another one of those delicious drinks and then the world kinda tilted.

"I think it's time I head home. Do you see my grandparents?" she had asked Henry as she scanned the room.

"I think Mr. and Mrs. Wyatt left a while ago. I can give you a ride if you'd like."

"That would be great. Thank you."

She had found her coat and Henry was escorting her to his car when Marshall came running out of the house.

"Henry! Dispatch called. Dinky just picked up old man Tabby again for trying to pee his name in the snow in the courthouse parking lot. He's in jail and is asking for his lawyer."

4

"Not again. Every winter I get these calls. But, I guess when your last name is Tabernacle, it takes a lot of tries to write that whole name out. I'll get him after I take Katelyn home."

"I can take her home. Tabby's throwing a major fit and giving Dinky all kinds of trouble at the jail. It's best you hurry. My deputy won't put up with it too much longer."

She had tried to protest, but had been shoved into the front seat of his Jeep before she could even form the words. She watched the way his black suit clung to his thighs and hips as he strode across the front of the car and to his door.

The car had gotten hot then. Thinking of the way they had danced and the way those thighs brushed against her. The way his hand wrapped around her waist. The feel of his hard, strong body as he pulled her tight against him.

Katelyn could almost feel him against her now. The way her body fit so perfectly into his. The way he warmed her from the inside. The way... Katelyn's eyes flew open and she bit the pillow to keep from screaming.

As her eyes focused all she could see was Marshall's naked chest, smattered with a dusting of brown hair over his well-defined muscles. She felt his arms around her and oh my God! She felt more than just his arms!

Panicked, her eyes darted around the masculine room. The curtains were open. The dark green sheets were scattered across the big bed. She tried to reach down and pull the covers up, but the pile of sheets groaned and a rust colored nose poked out, followed by a matching colored dog head. The dog looked at her and she would've sworn he laughed at her. He also refused to give up the covers.

Left with no choice, she slowly pulled away from Marshall. When she broke his hold she held her breath and waited for him to wake up. Luckily, he continued his deep sleep as she slid out of bed.

"Panties, where are my panties?" She whispered to herself.

At the sound of the dog's tail thumping on the bed, Katelyn looked up to see her black lace panties hanging from the dog's jowls.

"Good boy. Give me my panties." She reached for them just to have the dog turn his head away each time she tried to grab them. "Dammit! Keep them."

She slid the tight cream-colored sweater dress over her head and pulled on her brown suede boots before looking back to the bed. Marshall laid spread out on his bed. The only remaining covers laid low over his abdomen, one bare leg sticking out.

"What are you doing, Jacks?" She asked as she stared down at him. "Well, it wouldn't hurt to see what's under there. I mean it's not like I haven't seen it before, I just don't remember it."

Katelyn held her breath as her shaky fingers pulled down the sheet. Just a quick peek.

"Dammit."

Chapter One

K atelyn gasped and pressed all five foot ten inches of her
body against the old brick wall outside the Blossom Café.
She sucked in her belly and turned her face against the
warm brick. Silently she cursed the twenty pounds, okay, twenty-five
pounds, she put on since she retired from modeling as she tried to
become invisible.

All she had wanted was to get herself and her staff some lunch
from the Café, but of course *he* just had to be there. He was
everywhere. The Café, the grocery store, church, the Spring Fling
party — everywhere!

She slowly leaned sideways towards the large plate glass
window of the Café. First her shoulder, then her sharp chin, and
finally her pert nose passed the window until she could turn her eyes
to peek inside. Damn. He was leaning against the checkout counter
in his brown Sheriff's uniform. One hand rested lazily on the worn
wood counter as he talked to the Rose sisters. Ugh, he even had them
laughing. She rolled her eyes and looked again. It seemed like he was
in it for the long haul.

Katelyn put the back of her head against the wall and sighed. It
has been a challenge these past four months, but she had managed to
avoid him since that horrid one-night stand back in February.

It had been the shock of her life to open her eyes and find him
lying naked beside her. She wouldn't pretend to be an angel, but she

certainly had never had a one-night stand. What made it worse was the fact that the man she had the one-night stand with had been her secret crush who, for unknown reasons, despised her.

She had snuck out of his house in the early morning light as fast as she could, leaving Marshall naked and alone in bed. Even as she tried not to think about it, she couldn't stop her mind from flashing to the image of him in bed. His muscles, his face soft with sleep instead of tight with anger. It had been a hard thing to do, but she couldn't face the embarrassment of being there when he woke up. If he thought poorly of her before, she was definitely at the bottom of his list now. For reasons she didn't want to think of, this bothered her.

So, she simply pretended it hadn't happened. How was that working out? Not so well. She'd wake up hugging her pillow in the morning after a night of flashbacks. A kiss, a caress, she could feel him in her dreams and it was torture. But the torture didn't end there. Oh no, that would be too simple.

Her grandparents' cook's son had seen her doing the walk of shame back into Wyatt Estate at five in the morning. He had told his wife, who told her sister who works at the beauty salon, who told Miss Lily when she came in to get her hair permed. By nine o'clock in the morning it was all over town that Katelyn Jacks had come home the next morning wearing last night's clothes.

Speculation had run rampant. It followed her everywhere. People whispered and the Rose sisters had opened up a betting pool at the Blossom Café. To make matters worse, Red had to step down as Sheriff after suffering a bad case of pneumonia. Health problem after health problem had finally forced the old lawman out to pasture.

A special election was held and Marshall ran unopposed. The town couldn't stop talking about it. Their prodigal son returned to them, if you count working in Lexington thirty minutes away as leaving Keeneston. Posters with his face were in all of the windows showing their support for his candidacy. All of her clients were talking about him. She was trying to forget the night had even happened, but the town had a different idea.

After the election she thought it would get better. Wrong. It got worse! Now Marshall was walking around in his uniform and stepping over the girls who were swooning at his feet. Clients tittered to her all day long about how handsome he was. How they'd like to see what's under that uniform. All she could think about was that she *did* know what was under that uniform.

Then it got even worse. As if it wasn't bad enough having everyone in town speculate on whom she had spent the night with and the fact that every warm-blooded woman in the county was talking about wanting to see Marshall naked, there was Marshall himself. He was everywhere. She even had to duck behind a car when he slowly cruised down Main Street last week.

Well, enough was enough. She wasn't going to hide anymore. She was going to do the only thing she could think of — tuck tail and run.

Marshall smiled at a joke Miss Lily made as he waited for his lunch in the Blossom Café. He'd been Sheriff now for two months. He had never been so happy or so bored. He loved working in his hometown. But since he had taken office the only fun thing he'd done was bug Katelyn Jacks.

He had tried staying in his office like Red used to, but women were always dropping by with casseroles, cookies, and cakes. His office had turned into a bakery and all of his deputies were fighting over who got to sit in the front office to get the first chance at the single ladies of Keeneston. That left Annie Blake, well, Davies now to be in charge of Belle control. His sister-in-law would roll her eyes, snort, or just outright laugh at the women who happened to lock themselves out of their cars and needed rescuing by the Sheriff, especially the Keeneston Belles.

The Belles were a group of women who had their "coming out" at eighteen. They were a small and select group of women resembling debutants. However, unlike the debutants, the Belles were an even smaller and even more exclusive group. To be a Belle, you had to be a debutant, graduate high school with honors, be single, and resolve to be married by the age of twenty-five to only the best and the brightest from Keeneston. They also had to be of a certain socioeconomic level, so to say. It didn't hurt either to be named prom queen. But, the real kicker was at least three generations of women in your family had to be Belles.

The Belles were husband hunters extraordinaire and had had the Davies men in their sights since they came back from overseas. The brothers had been so messed up after all they had seen and done in the course of war that the last thing they had wanted was a wife. They had become experts at outmaneuvering and, well, frankly, hiding from the Belles. Maybe that was why Cy was M.I.A. — he was trying to hide from the Belles.

But now the Belles were getting desperate to nab one of the Davies brothers. The first one had fallen. Cade had gone and married a smart talking, kick ass, DEA Agent. The Belles had gasped and redoubled their efforts. Miles and Pierce were in Lexington a lot, so that left Marshall in their sights. Hopefully now that Pierce had just graduated with a Master in Agriculture he'd be around more to take the heat off of Marshall.

So, Marshall had had no choice. He stuck Annie out front, much to her dissatisfaction. Just the other month, Annie had announced that both she and Marshall's sister Paige were going to make him an Uncle. They were both due within a week of each other around Christmas. So, Marshall had played the pregnancy card. With a huff, she'd guard him from the Keeneston Belles and all the other single, and sometimes not so single, women of Keeneston. That worked well for a while, but then he had come out once when he heard yelling. Annie had her stun gun drawn and was reading the riot act to Nancy Kincaid, who was in the process of trying to climb over the counter, all while balancing a plate of her famous oatmeal cookies in one hand. The week before it had been Jasmine Franklin. She and Nancy were the two most persistent of the Belles.

He had decided then he didn't want to be at fault for Annie going to jail over shooting one of them, so he went mobile. He cruised around town, he walked the streets, and he spent a lot of time at the Cafe. While the Rose sisters, Lily Rae, Daisy Mae, and Violet Fae wanted him married, they at least weren't part of the Belles, or the Keeneston Ladies Club, which a Belle graduated to once she was married. The Ladies Club had their hand in everything. Their husbands ranged from the Judge, to the D.A., to the Mayor, and of course every one of those men listened to their wives. Further, they sat on all the important town committees.

The Rose sisters suggested single women, pointed out how happy his brother Cade and sister Paige were now they were married and expecting, but they always kept the Belles in line. The Rose sisters didn't need a club or a husband to run the town. And the Belles and the Ladies Club both knew that.

"I still think it was Henry," Miss Lily whispered to him.

Marshall shook his head and looked at three faces staring at him. "I'm sorry, what?"

"I bet it was Henry that Katelyn spent the night with back in February."

"That's silly Lily Rae," said Miss Violet. "Henry would've been braggin' about it non-stop. No, I think it was Paul Russell. He was real interested in Kenna when she came to town, and I bet he'd be very interested in Katelyn. Especially since Kenna was snatched up so quickly by Will. He's surely smooth enough in that political way. So, who do you think? You took her home, didn't you?"

Miss Violet leveled a steely gaze at Marshall, just as she had been doing for the past four months. Although with her being so short and round and generally rosy cheeked, it was hard to be too intimidated.

"I dropped her off safe and sound. What she did after that is her own business." He didn't mention he dropped her off safe and sound at his own house. Or the fact that he had had his fair share of one night stands, especially the year after he came home, but none had affected him the way one night in Katelyn's arms had. Or the fact that he had figured out the one woman in town not trying to get his attention was the only one he couldn't stop thinking about.

"Speak of the devil. Just what do you think she's doing out there?" Miss Daisy leaned her thin, steely, body over the counter and openly stared at the shoulder of one Katelyn Jacks pressed against the side of the window.

The bell rang and Roger Burns, the great-uncle of Paul Russell, came hobbling into the Cafe. His cane thumped slowly as he made his way to an open table. He took off his bowler hat to expose the thin white hair combed neatly over his shiny pink head.

"I'll tell you what. I don't understand young people these days. That purdy lady vet is out there pressed against the wall. Doesn't she know you have to come inside to eat?"

Ah! His day just got brighter. Marshall had to admit, he was having a lot of fun tormenting Katelyn. There was nothing that made him laugh harder than to see her dive behind a car when she saw him coming.

"Well, I better get to work. I'm just going to head out the back door and start my patrol. Thanks for the lunch ladies."

He walked through the kitchen and quietly went out the back door to the gravel parking lot. He turned left and went down the alley to reach the street. He was going to sneak up on the only woman to ever sneak out of his bed.

He reached the street and turned toward Main Street. Marshall had known what he was doing the second he saw Henry getting ready to take her home. The jealousy had been instantaneous. Paige had always teased him and his brothers about not wanting a toy until another boy played with it, but this was more. It went straight to his gut and turned it to stone at the thought of Henry, um, playing with her.

The thing that had confused him was that he didn't know where the jealousy had come from. He didn't even like the spoiled brat.

Katelyn had always come and visited her grandparents every summer when she was a kid. She was younger than him, probably by four or five years, but she had acted as if she was already thirty. She was always in these ridiculous dresses, even when she was playing. Well, as much playing as a hotel heiress with everything in life handed to her did.

When she got tired of playing dress up with her dolls, she decided to play dress up herself and became a model. She'd been sucked up to, spoiled, and hadn't worked a day in her life.

She may still look like she could belong on the runway, but even he knew that it was tough to make it in the modeling world when she was approaching her late twenties. So she came home now to play doctor. What was pissing him off to no end was that he couldn't stop the desire that hit him every time he saw her.

It still bugged him that when he had taken her home that night, he had fully intended to be the one gone in the morning. It was an asshole move to leave her alone in his house, but he was hoping it would cure his fascination with her. Instead just the opposite happened.

He had woken up happy. He had slept comfortably for the first time since he was deployed overseas. Most of the time, he still woke up once or twice a night from a memory, the sound of gunfire, the sound of death. But this time he woke up happy and refreshed. He reached for her only to find Bob, Marshall's dog, lying with his head on the pillow instead of Katelyn.

But now she was right around the corner from him. He was giddy at the chance of tormenting her further. He'd just pretend that was the only reason he was giddy and ignore the fact he couldn't wait to be near her again. Marshall put on his best cop face and turned the corner. Disappointment pushed his shoulders down to a slump. She was gone.

Chapter Two

Katelyn loved everything about Wyatt Farm. She stopped at the elaborate iron gate and pressed the opener. As the large scrolled gate opened, she looked down the long narrow paved driveway lined with Bradford pear trees. She headed down the shaded drive looking at the colts and fillies of her grandparents' farm romping in pastures that surrounded the main house.

On top of a small hill sat Wyatt Estate. The old farmhouse had stood in the same place since 1785. Her relatives had moved to Keeneston after the Rose family and one or two other families, but were still considered to be one of the first families of Keeneston. However, unlike most of the other first families, they had chosen to farm the land. They settled on a large tract of land on the far side of the county. Granted, the county was small, like most other counties in Kentucky, but at the time they were considered on the frontier.

They had chosen wisely. Their property contained a creek and an underground water source. They had grown various vegetables that the grocery store in town sold, and tobacco they sold directly to old Irish and British contacts. They also raised sheep for wool, cows for milking, pigs, and racehorses. They were completely self-sufficient.

Katelyn's ancestors on her grandfather's side had started off as poor migrant farmers from Ireland when they migrated to Virginia in the 1770's to avoid the stranglehold on trade that Britain was imposing. They had fallen in love with the idea of freedom and packed up everything they had and headed for the new world.

They arrived during a period of tense buildup between the colonies and Great Britain. Soon the American Revolution broke out. The men picked up arms and fought for their freedom while the women in the family packed all their belongings once again. While her great grandfather many times over fought in the Revolution for the Virginia Colony, his wife single-handedly made her way to the new town of Lexington in the frontier part of Virginia that would soon become Kentucky.

When the war was over, her husband found her there and they pushed even farther into the untamed wilds of the frontier. They settled in Keeneston, north of Fort Harrod, the first permanent settlement this far out on in the wilderness. Her family built a small log cabin in 1780 and then started construction on the main house. It took them five years to build it. They sold food to the growing town of Lexington to finance the building supplies and were able to move into their large three-story rectangular shaped brick house five years later.

Every generation since then added something to the house. Beautiful rose gardens, indoor plumbing, lighting, garage, sunroom and so on as technology advanced. But, the bones of the house were still original and she felt as if the house was alive with her history. As if it breathed and told the story of their lives.

Her grandfather had taken over the farm upon his graduation from Emory University in Atlanta. He had come back home with a young wife in hand. Her grandmother belonged to an old family that had their ancestral home forty minutes outside Atlanta. They had met at a party and it was love at first sight.

Katelyn parked her car in front of the large white brick house and opened the old thick front door. She padded quickly across the tongue and groove pine floors that were polished high and into the updated kitchen. A large screened in patio with a brick floor and overstuffed elegant white wicker furniture sat off the backside of the kitchen.

Katelyn loved to grab a sandwich out of the fridge and sit there overlooking the farmland. That was her plan until she found her grandparents already sitting on the porch.

"Katelyn! Dear, what a pleasant surprise." Her grandmother, Ruth Wyatt, stood up elegantly from the chair.

Her grandmother was her favorite person in the world. More like a mother to her really. She loved the fact that it seemed her grandparents belonged in a different era where men rode around on stallions and rescued damsels in distress. Nana wore a pale yellow muslin dress today. Her face was on and complete with her customary bright red lipstick.

"Hi Nana. I was just coming home to grab some lunch. Hi Papa." She leaned down and gave her grandfather a kiss on the cheek.

Beauford Wyatt was still a vision. His tall lean frame was always in a three-piece suit, even though he lived out on a farm. He may still dabble in racehorses and farming, but in reality that was all her grandmother. Her grandfather was an investment banker. He was technically retired and didn't go into the office in Lexington every day, but it didn't mean he didn't work anymore. He had his office here at the farm and ran the family trusts and accounts as well for some of his friends.

"Your Nana was just plotting out your life, darlin'. I thought you might want a say in it though."

"Nana? Plotting my life again?" she teased.

"Well, you know I didn't say anything when you dated that horrid photographer. Or when you dated that sleazy actor, or the insipid male model you did that brilliant cover shoot with... but at least you were dating."

"Nana, I have a pretty good memory, and I definitely remember you saying something bad about each of my old boyfriends," she grinned.

Her Nana had spoken her mind about each and every one of them and had been right. But, they were years ago. When she was out of the limelight and in the labs at Auburn, those type guys didn't knock on her door anymore. Instead she got gross professors and stupid jocks that thought dating her was all about them and their status. Like she cared if the quarterback for the football team could take her anywhere. She'd been to places all on her own that were a lot more interesting. She had no desire to be a trophy wife. That had "bad reality show" written all over it.

"Humph, well, it was better than not dating anyone at all. You work too hard and that doesn't leave much room for fun."

"I have to work hard to afford the payments on my clinic. I just bought over a million dollars' worth of equipment."

"Pish posh. You know you have that in your bank account if you want it. You don't think I know about how much money you made as a model, and then there was your perfume and that clothing line you just sold to Bloomingdales. This is about you not wanting to get out there and get hurt again."

"Nana! Were you snooping in Papa's office again?"

With an elegant wave of her hand, her grandmother dismissed the question.

"You need a good country boy. Don't give me that look. Not all country boys are dumb rednecks. Look at your grandfather. Look at, say, Miles Davies or any of his brothers. Marshall ran his own security firm before taking over as Sheriff, you know."

She felt her cheeks redden. She couldn't escape Marshall even at home. The trouble was every time she heard his name she couldn't help but remember the way he felt against her body as they moved on the dance floor, and as they moved together somewhere else.

"Nana! Marshall is just a stupid country boy who happens to have connections. He would be horrible to date. I'm sure one of the Belles will make a perfect trophy wife for him someday."

"Now don't talk bad about the Belles! You know you could've been one. You can still be a Keeneston Lady when you get married."

"I need to get to work. I'll see you tonight. And no more life planning!"

She placed a kiss on her grandparents' cheeks and headed back to her car with an armful of food she snagged from the pantry for her staff.

Katelyn took a seat in the soft rolling desk chair behind the computer at the receptionist's desk and smiled. She wiggled her toes inside her Crocs and wiped her hands on her blue scrubs. She had just completed a successful operation to remove a tumor on the thyroid gland of a six-year-old border collie. She had shelled out the money for a laser and it had worked like a dream.

Shelly Duffy came back up to her desk and put a hip on the corner. Shelly had been her one friend from when she was younger. She was happily married to her high school sweetheart and had an eight-year-old daughter. Her light brown hair was pulled back into a ponytail. Her motherly attitude brought peace and comfort to the clinic.

They were always the odd couple. Katelyn had been tall and boney as a child and Shelly had been short and pleasantly plump. Katelyn had been wealthy and Shelly grew up in the Keeneston Trailer Park.

As soon as Katelyn knew she was going to open her clinic, she knew she wanted Shelly with her. Shelly was thrilled. She was working the night shift at a bourbon distillery and wanted to be able to spend more time with her family. Katelyn gave her the job and the two of them got the clinic up and running in no time. She'd be lost without Shelly up front doing all the check-ins and keeping up with the billing.

"Did you hear the news?" Shelly asked full of excitement.

"What news?"

"The Keeneston Most Eligible list came out in this week's paper."

Katelyn watched in fear as Shelly opened one of the drawers and pulled out the newspaper. It was worse than Page Six when she lived in New York City.

"You're the number one most eligible lady!"

"Me?"

"That's right. Ew, Nancy Kinkaid is second. She's such a... well, my manners prevent me from saying what I think about her. Yummy! Miles Davies is number one. Marshall is number two. I bet that's some hot sibling rivalry. Maybe they have naked pillow fights?"

Katelyn just rolled her eyes at her friend.

"Yeah, you're right. But they probably go horseback riding without their shirts." Shelly sighed.

Katelyn had to sigh too. She'd seen Marshall without a shirt and imagining his muscles in the sun as he rode toward her gave her a hot flash.

"Who else made the guy's list?"

"Paul Russell is third. I guess I get that, but I think it's just because he's the newly elected head councilman. I mean, he is handsome in that preppy way. He's just never wrinkled, you know?" Shelly asked rhetorically. "Fourth is Ahmed and there is nothing sexier than dark and dangerous. The best thing that happened in Keeneston was when our dear Prince Mohtadi came to town with his head of security! Mo and Dani are a cute couple and so down to earth, aren't they?" Shelly didn't give Katelyn a chance to respond before continuing, "Mo is elegant and has that royal carriage, but Ahmed is sinful."

"Who's fifth?" Katelyn asked, even though she secretly agreed about Ahmed.

"Fifth place is Henry Rooney."

"Pretty good top five. Henry is really sweet in a boyish way. I bet he's thrilled with being named a top bachelor. I can hear the pickup lines now!" Katelyn laughed.

"Oh, and if I'm not mistaken, here comes Bachelor Number Four. Unless you know someone else who drives a black Mercedes like that." Shelly sighed as she leaned closer to the window for a better look.

"Oh my gosh! Shelly, page the back and tell them to get the operating room up and ready. We have an emergency!"

Without hesitation, Shelly grabbed the intercom and Katelyn bolted out the door. She had seen Ahmed slide out of the car in his black suit and open the back door. He had bent down and when he straightened he had a dog in his arms. A dog that was a bloody mess and not moving.

"What happened?" she asked as she reached for her stethoscope hanging around her neck.

"I was doing a security sweep of the farm. I found him stuck in between the fence boards. He was breathing, but non-responsive. I pulled off the board and brought him straight here."

"He's breathing, but there are several spots that are going to need stitches and the dark bruising there on his stomach indicates that he's probably bleeding internally too. Quick, follow me."

Katelyn jumped up the two stairs and past Shelly who was already holding the front door open. She went through the "employees only" door and down the hall to the operating room.

"Put him here." She nodded her head to the sterile stainless steel table.

Her one technician was already holding a sterilized gown open for her to step into. Dottie tied it and held out the latex gloves for her. Katelyn shoved her hands in them and started an exam. She lifted the dog's lips and pressed her finger on the gum line. The pale gums and lack of color flooding to where she pressed was just another sign of probable internal bleeding.

"Dottie, tube him. I need him under for a while. I think we're going to have to go in."

Dottie's head bobbed under the blue surgical cap that covered her honey-colored hair. You couldn't get Dottie to shut up any other time, but during emergencies she was a miracle worker.

Dottie guided the plastic tube to the dog's trachea and turned on the anesthetic while Katelyn palpitated the abdomen and then looked over the other wounds.

"There's a bad one on his neck. Looks like a dog went for his neck and tried to rip it out. Dottie, start cleaning that and I'll look at it in a minute. I need to get inside. Mr. Ahmed, you may want to wait outside."

Ahmed simply raised an eyebrow and didn't budge from the doorway.

"Okay, but this is going take a while," Katelyn said as she slid the sharp scalpel down the dog's stomach.

"What do you see, Dottie?" She asked as she worked her way into the dog's abdomen.

"It's pretty bad. I clamped off one of the bleeds for you. I'm suturing what I can."

"Okay. The belly is full of blood. I need suction." Katelyn planted her feet and readied herself for the long haul.

Three hours later Katelyn tied off the last suture. Her scrubs were soaked through with sweat. She ripped off her mask and hair covering as she gave the dog one last going over.

"Okay. Dottie, go prepare run number three for him and I'll wash him up a little before I bring him back there."

"Let me help you, he must weigh close to a hundred pounds," Ahmed finally said.

He had stood by the doorway the whole three hours and never made a sound. In fact she forgot he was even there. She looked up to him now and saw the tight line of his mouth and the worried crease in his forehead underneath his black hair. His hands were relaxed by his side, but his compact body radiated with energy.

"It's alright Mr. Ahmed. I can get him."

"Please, just Ahmed is fine. What happened to him?"

Katelyn watched as he straightened up to his full height and came towards the table. He was about her height, had massive shoulders and a muscular chest that narrowed slightly into his waist. He looked like he could carry the dog, her, and Dottie as if it were nothing.

His strong hand, riddled with small white-lined scars rested on the dog's wide head and slowly stroked it. Katelyn was surprised by his gentle touch and obvious concern for the dog. It was completely unexpected.

"Looks like this dog lost a fight."

"A fight?"

"Yes. These are classic injuries from a dog fight—a professional dog fight. Not Muffy and Puffy getting into a fight over their dinner."

She watched as his jaw tightened and his dark brown eyes flashed with anger. He pulled out his cell phone and hit a number as he walked out the door. Well, he was a man of few words.

Katelyn finished cleaning the wounds and rechecked his gums. Still pale, but doing much better after getting a transfusion from her own dog, a white standard poodle named Ruffles. She was just about to carry the dog to the run when Ahmed came back into the room.

"I've ordered a full investigation. If there is anything on Mo's property that is evidence of a dog-fighting ring, I'll know about it by the morning. Here, let me."

As she expected, he effortlessly lifted the dog off the operating table. She watched in awe as he brought the dog to his chest and quietly whispered to him in a language she didn't understand.

"Right this way." She led him down another hall and into the kennel. "Rebekah will be on duty tonight. She'll watch over him and call me if anything changes. The next day will decide if he's going to make it or not."

"Can I give you my number? I know it's late and your receptionist went home already. But, if anything happens, I'd like to know. I will also pay all the bills for him."

"I'm not worried about that. I am worried about the internal bleeding. But yes, give me your number and I'll call you with an update."

She pulled out her phone and handed it over to him. He typed in his name and number and handed it back.

"Can I stay here with him for a while? I want to make sure he wakes up."

"Sure. I have work to do around here and will check back in an hour or so."

"I can't find Caesar." Camille Watkins wrung her thin hands together as she looked at her husband.

"What do you mean, you can't find Caesar? The dog was half dead!"

Andre Watkins was a large man. He was a tough man and he was not a happy man right now. The tattoo of a pinup woman on his biceps danced as he tried to control his anger by clinching his hand into a fist over and over again.

"Don't yell at me, you're the one who thought to use him for training with Antony."

"We can't have anything go wrong, especially now. We've worked too hard to get here. I'm going to find him. Just let the regional director know the fight went off well tonight. That the winner walked away with eight thousand and regionals made another ten thousand. That'll make him happy. But, for God's sake, don't tell him about Caesar."

Andre grabbed a spare leash from the dirty floor of their training shed and headed out into the woods with his flashlight. He had to find that damn dog before someone else did.

★　　★　　★

Katelyn looked up from her paperwork and saw it was already ten o'clock at night. She stretched her legs and grabbed her stethoscope. She'd do rounds and then check on the pit bull. If everything were alright she'd go home and get some sleep before coming back and checking on him early in the morning.

She made her way to the runs and found Ahmed sitting on the floor of the run with the dog. She couldn't help but smile at his kindness. He had wrapped the dog up in a blanket and rested the dog's big head in his lap. He was quietly talking to him while gently stroking his head.

"How's our patient?" She asked as she listened to his heart.

The dog opened his eyes and looked at her. She felt his body tense, but at Ahmed's quiet words, she felt the dog relax once again.

"I don't know much about dogs, but he's awake. He was cold when he came out of the anesthetic and very scared. Whoever did this deserves a slow and painful death."

She quietly agreed, but was a little worried by his cold and deadly serious tone that if she said it out loud he may actually do it.

"His vitals are improving. I'll give him another round of pain medication and then see how he's doing in a couple of hours. But, now, I'm going home."

"Let me walk you to the car." Ahmed stood and the dog whimpered. "It's alright Zoticus, I will be back to see you in the morning. This nice lady is going to take care of you tonight." He looked to Bekah and Katelyn almost rolled her eyes at the dreamy grin on Bekah's face.

"Zoticus?" She asked as they walked outside.

"It's Latin for 'full of life.'"

"That is a great name for him. I'll put it on his chart tomorrow." Katelyn reached her car and tossed in her purse. "I will call you if anything changes."

"Thank you, Doctor. You were amazing tonight. You have a special gift."

Katelyn blushed and was glad for the dark parking lot. She climbed into her car and looked up at him.

"Good night, Ahmed."

"Good night."

Marshall warmed up a slice of leftover pizza and scooped out a bowl of dog food for his vizsla, Bob. The doorbell stopped him from sitting down at the kitchen table. Looking at his watch, he hoped eleven at night was too late for the Belles to be locked out and wanting to be rescued or for them to just be stopping by.

"Jesus, what the hell happened to you?" he asked as he took in the sight of Ahmed covered in blood.

"Hello Marshall. Can I come in?"

"Of course, do I need to call an ambulance?"

"No need. Not my blood."

"In that case, I was just about to eat my… Bob!" His plate was empty and his solid rust colored dog sat in his chair as if it was his. "That was my pizza. How many times do I have to tell you, you're a dog! You eat dog food and you eat it on the floor."

"I don't think your dog believes you."

"I don't either. I've only been trying to tell him for the past four years, but he thinks I'm full of shit. I don't know if he's ever actually eaten dog food."

"Your dog frightens me. The way he looks at us, I think he believes he's smarter than us," Ahmed said as Bob rolled his eyes at him and then licked his lips.

"He may be right. So, you going to tell me what's going on?"

"I found a dog near death trying to get onto our property. He had managed to crawl halfway through the fence before getting stuck. I rushed him to Katelyn, I mean, Dr. Jacks. It took her three hours of surgery to stop all the bleeding."

"Wow. What caused it?"

"Dr. Jacks believes the dog was a loser in a professional dog fight. I thought as Sheriff you'd want to know."

"I do. Thank you. I didn't know we had any dog-fighting rings around here. I'll contact the humane societies and some of my cop friends and see what I can find out."

"I'm running an investigation of my own on the farm. If we find any evidence you'll be the first call I make. But, I've got to say, Dr. Jacks is something else. I'm glad I saw that stupid Bachelor/Bachelorette list and remembered she was here. I don't think old Doc Truett would've been able to save Zoticus."

"Zoticus?"

"That's the name I picked for the dog. Dr. Jacks was so focused during the surgery. She was amazing," Ahmed said with reverence.

"I'm sure she was," he said dryly. That damn list. He didn't want anyone else thinking she was amazing. That was his secret.

Chapter Three

Katelyn's eyes shot open. Grrr. She was too wired about the surgery to fall asleep. She always was when her patients were still in the woods. She rolled over in bed and looked at the clock. Three minutes past three in the morning. All of two minutes had passed since she last looked at the clock.

She kicked the covers off and found a new pair of scrubs. She slid her feet into a pair of sneakers and put her long straight hair into a ponytail without looking in the mirror. She walked quietly down the hall then down the old squeaky steps. If she couldn't sleep, she might as well check on Zoticus instead.

The drive to the clinic was a short one. She loved seeing the small building all lit up, even in the middle of the night. She had made the right choice in hiring Rebekah on as night staff. She just felt better having someone there with the animals. She parked near the front door. Bekah's car was parked around the building in the staff parking lot, but there were no lights back there and Katelyn had learned the hard way to use the front door. She had tripped over a root and fallen into a tree. She felt brilliant for that.

She opened her car door and headed past the dog walk area towards the front door. She unlocked the front door and unarmed the alarm.

"Bekah! It's just me," she yelled as she made her way through the waiting room.

"Back at the cages," she heard Bekah yell.

Katelyn made her way through the exam room and the area behind them to the cages and runs.

"How's our boy doing?"

"He's doing pretty well. Mr. Ahmed called already to check on him. His color is doing well and he's perking up more. He's very scared and subsequently somewhat aggressive."

Katelyn looked in at the dog and was relieved to see him so alert. By the way his eyes were darting around she could tell he was scared and unsure of his environment. She went over to the dog food bins and pulled out a handful of food.

She kept her hand closed and slightly outstretched as she confidently approached the cage. In low, soft tones, she talked to the dog and presented her hand to the wire separating them. The dog raised his head and sniffed the air, never taking his eyes off of her. She reached over and unlatched the run and stepped inside. The dog continued to eye her and tense in fear as she approached, but didn't make any other moves. She bent down and paused, allowing the dog to get accustomed to her.

She took a kibble of food and rolled it over to him. The dog's tongue greedily shot out and ate it. She rolled another kibble of food and watched it vanish. She came closer and repeated the process until he was scarfing food out of the palm of her hand. He was now relaxed and the excitement of meeting someone new was obviously wearing on him. She did a quick exam and, happy with the results, pulled the blanket back over him and let him go to sleep after giving him a quick rub behind his ears.

"He looks good. I'm surprised. I thought he wouldn't make it."

"He sure likes you. I wonder how long it has been since he ate."

"I think he ate just enough to live on. It's clear whoever owned him wasn't bulking him up. But the way his ribs are sticking out says he hasn't eaten recently. Well, now that I know he's doing well, I'm going to try to get a couple of hours of sleep."

Katelyn said goodnight and headed toward the front door. She made sure to set the alarm and lock the door. She was halfway to her car when she sensed movement. She froze and looked around.

A shadow leapt from the tree in the dog walk area, hitting her hard in the stomach. She felt her breath being forced from her lungs as she fell backwards. She landed on her back in the grass and felt her body reverberate before pain shot through her head as it crashed into the ground.

Katelyn was dizzy and couldn't focus on the people lying on top of her. She squinted and the two people became one man with a black mask. Fear shot through her as her heart stopped. What was she supposed to do? She had taken a self-defense class, but she couldn't remember a single thing right now but to scream.

Katelyn grunted and gasped as the heavy man shifted to straddle her. His arm pushed her shoulder into the ground that was wet with dew. She opened her mouth and tried to find the breath to scream, but a cold, leather-gloved hand came down over her mouth. Her nostrils flared as she tried to get some air into her lungs. Her chest burned, her head swam, and she felt as if she was suffocating.

The glint of steel caught her attention as he waved a wide hunting knife in front of her face.

"What's the code? What's the fucking code?" He growled.

Katelyn's eyes went wide and she couldn't understand what he wanted. She shook her head and looked into the black mask.

"For the clinic you dumb bitch. You got Ketamine in there?"

"What?"

"Ketamine? I'm sure you do. Probably some codeine too. Now, you're going to get up, unlock the door and turn off the alarm. Then you're going to unlock the medicine cabinet for me. If you do all that, then I'll let you live. Nod if you understand."

Katelyn nodded and let go of the death grip she had on his arm. Her eyes darted toward the door to make sure Bekah wasn't in view. What would this guy do when he realized there was someone else in the clinic? As she looked toward the door a metallic shine caught her eye.

"Yeah, I have Ketamine, but not very much. What else were you looking for?"

Katelyn stretched her arm slowly toward the object. Her middle finger felt its cold strength as she wrapped one finger after another around it.

"Codeine, and I bet you have some steroids too."

She nodded as her hand closed around it and she prayed it would be enough. As the man started to stand up she swung the pooper-scooper as hard as she could. The pooper-scooper cut through the air, landing hard against the side of his face.

"Shit!" He cursed as he stumbled backward, falling onto the ceramic fire hydrant in the dog walk area.

"No kidding," she mumbled as she jumped up and ran for the front door. She scooped up her keys that had gone flying when she was tackled and plunged them into the lock.

"Dr. Jacks?" Bekah called from the back.

"We're being robbed!"

"Not while I'm here." Bekah came through the door with a .38 caliber revolver drawn.

"Where did that come from?"

Bekah turned off the alarm and then rearmed it before going to the window. "I work nights. Of course I have a gun! I don't see anyone."

Katelyn inched her way to the window and looked out. She scanned the tree line and didn't see the man who attacked her or any shadows lurking behind trees.

"You want me to call the Sheriff?" Bekah asked as she reached for the phone.

Katelyn lunged, shoving her body between Bekah and the phone.

"No! We don't want to disturb them. Unfortunately, this thing happens to vet clinics. Drug addicts think we're an easy mark. It's why we have the alarm. Besides, he's gone now and he had a mask on. I couldn't tell them anything except that he had a barbwire tattoo around the lower part of his neck. Something I'm sure is common in the drug world."

"True. My boyfriend has one around his arm and he's not even a drug dealer. Well, I'll stay at the door and watch you get to your car. I'll call if there are any more problems."

"Thanks Bekah. Good night."

Marshall picked up his pace. She was right behind him and closing in for the kill. The door was getting closer, just a couple more steps. He picked up his black boots and dove through the door to the Blossom Café just before Nancy could catch up to him.

"Afternoon, Sheriff. You want some lunch to go with your gossip?" Miss Daisy asked as she set a glass of lemonade down in front of Shelly Duffy.

"You know I don't gossip," he said as he took a seat at what had become known as his table.

He also knew that was a big fat fib. Half of his job was listening to gossip and calming situations before something could come of it. Just the other week he prevented the theft of old man Tabby's champion pig. The seniors thought it would be funny to steal the pig and let it loose in the school as the teachers were getting their final grades in.

"Humph." Miss Daisy set a glass of water down on the table and turned back to Shelly. "Do you think they're dating?"

"I don't think so. I mean, he was there because of his dog," Shelly shrugged before taking a sip of her drink.

"I heard he was there with her until late at night, like Jay Leno late. That's not being there just because of some dog he just found," Pam Gilbert said before taking a bite of her salad.

"I heard he was there late too. And when he heard she was attacked, he vowed to protect her...personally," Miss Violet called out from the kitchen.

"Ahmed could protect me personally any day of the week and twice on Fridays," Shelly sighed dreamily.

"I hear that. They'd make one handsome couple, our Katelyn and Ahmed," Miss Daisy said as she put a hot brown sandwich down in front of Shelly.

"What!" Marshall almost bolted out of his seat.

He didn't know which to be more upset about, Katelyn being attacked last night and not calling him or the fact she was now dating Ahmed. Either way it now gave him a good excuse to go over and see her and find out how much of the truth was mixed in the hearty helping of gossip he just got served.

Katelyn slammed her fingers down on the keyboard as she filled out her doctor's notes on the aptly named twenty-three pound cat, Mr. Tubs. Shelly had just gotten back from lunch and told her the café was abuzz with the gossip that she and Ahmed were dating. Okay, if she were being honest, it wouldn't be the worst thing in the world.

Of course, since she knew Shelly so well, Katelyn was pretty sure she helped the gossip along. But, what really got to her was what Shelly had said about Marshall's reaction. She also informed her that Marshall would probably be here in the next ten minutes. She didn't want to have to explain anything to Marshall and she didn't want to listen to a lecture about Ahmed or the attempted burglary. She was sore, she was tired, and dammit, she wasn't going to take it anymore.

She gave a little fist pump, looked at her watch and ducked out the back door. It looked like she'd take lunch at home and hopefully her one o'clock would forgive her for being a little late.

Katelyn felt herself relax the second she turned into Wyatt Farm. Her grandparents' farm always had a sense of peace about it. The horses frolicking in the pastures, the shaded lane, the red, yellow, purple and white flowers her Nana had planted all around the farm, and the pearl pink Lincoln Town Car bounding through the pasture.

The what? Nana always drove her car through the pastures to say hello to every horse on the farm. She had a bag of peppermints in the car and would give every single horse one. However, she wasn't driving at her normally sedate speed of slightly faster than a snail. No, she was flying. The car was even taking air as it flew over small hills. Her eyes widened as she watched Nana slam on the brakes, sliding the car into park.

Something was dreadfully wrong. Maybe it was one of the horses. She quickly parked behind her grandmother's car and raced into the house behind Nana's disheveled form.

"Beauford! Oh Beauford!" She heard her grandma yell from the foyer.

"What is it Sweet Pea?" her grandfather said from his nearby office.

"Oh Beauford! It was positively horrid! I've never been so vexed in all my life." Her grandmother's agitated voice reached her as she made her way towards her grandfather's office.

"Sweet Pea! You're bleeding! What happened? Are you all right, my dear?"

Katelyn stopped trying to eavesdrop and ran for her grandfather's office. She slid on the polished wood as she skidded to a stop at the open door. Her grandmother was sitting in one of the leather chairs; her long, billowy white dress was wrinkled and stained with blood dripping from a gash on the backside of her head.

"Nana! Oh my God!" She hurried to her grandmother's side and looked at her pale face. Her make-up was smeared and her hair out of place. That fact scared her more than the blood.

"I was attacked! I was attacked on our own property. Beauford, I've never been so angry!"

"What can I do, Nana?"

"You can call that nice young Sheriff and tell him to come out here, if you don't mind. I think I need to have a word with him," her grandmother said, her calm southern demeanor falling back into place.

Her grandmother's hand covered hers and gave it a pat. She was afraid it would be ice cold, but it was actually warm and color was flooding back to her face. She was getting angry. She had never seen her grandmother angry a day in her life, and from the look of it, she never wanted to be on the receiving end of that.

Katelyn stood and resolutely headed for the phone. The day she had dreaded for the past four months was finally here. She needed Marshall's help.

Chapter Four

Marshall took a bite of the meatloaf sandwich at the Blossom Café and brooded. He had waited at the clinic for fifteen minutes only to be told that the doc went out for lunch. That was now the second time she had snuck out on him.

"Dispatch to Sheriff. Do you copy?" Annie's voice crackled out from his radio.

"Yea, what do you need?"

"Katelyn Jacks just called 9-1-1!" Along with his heart stopping, so did all the conversation in the Café as everyone leaned closer to hear. "Mrs. Wyatt has been attacked and you're needed at the farm."

Gasps of shock and outrage filled the café as Marshall shoved his chair back. Two attacks on the same family in twelve hours. What was going on?

"Quick, Violet put up the closed sign!"

Marshall ignored the rush of people heading to their cars as he darted across the street to his cruiser parked in the courthouse parking lot. Mrs. Wyatt was eccentric, but she was a sweet and well-loved eccentric. By now the phone lines would be on fire with the news and most people would be grabbing spare casseroles and cakes out of their freezers and heading over to the farm.

This settled things. Katelyn was going to get protection if she wanted it or not. And come hell or high water, he was going to be the one to give it to her.

Marshall felt as if he were leading a processional. He flew down the country road with a line of cars right on his tail. He looked around the farm as he pulled to a stop behind Katelyn's car. Mrs. Wyatt's car had just missed a rose bush and was sitting at an angle by the front door.

He did a quick study of the surrounding property, but all he saw were people from the town parking their cars and the workers from the farm gathering. He'd have to talk to them after he found out what happened.

Marshall strode up to the door and pushed the doorbell and waited. Katelyn opened the door with a surgical glove on one hand and a drawn look to her face.

"Um, *we're* here to see how Mrs. Wyatt is doing. I'm here to investigate." He stepped forward when she opened the door. She didn't say anything and she didn't look him in the eye.

"Look Sweet Pea, the whole town came to check on you," Beauford said as he stepped up to the door.

"Beauford! Get my lipstick. I can't let them see me without my face on!" Mrs. Wyatt called from the office.

Marshall stepped farther through the door. He brushed by Katelyn and enjoyed the pleasure of feeling her stiffen.

"Dr. Jacks," he murmured. He didn't know where the husky tone of his voice came from. But by the way she became ramrod straight, he didn't question it. He just enjoyed it.

"Sheriff. My grandmother is in here. Please follow me."

He looked around at the historic old home. He had only been in it once or twice when Mrs. Wyatt allowed the schools to bring the kids through for a history lesson. Her family had all been supporters of the South. Most of her great-great aunts were named Dixie. She had period paintings, furniture, and memorabilia from the time. Sherman had actually burned her house as he made his march on Atlanta. When the family had heard he was coming, they had buried what they could, packed up and traveled westward until the end of the war as the men went off to fight. As they rebuilt they dug up what was left behind. Mrs. Wyatt had some of those artifacts hanging on her walls and decorating her house.

Her home still reflected that love of history as he caught a glimpse of an old rifle mounted over a fireplace in a sitting room. He turned into Beauford's office and saw Mrs. Wyatt looking like a bright red ghost.

"Oh, Sheriff, I'm so glad you're here!" She didn't bother to get up, but he didn't expect her to.

He went over to her and took her hand. She was still shaking a little, but seemed to be in control of her emotions now.

"Can you tell me what happened?"

"Well, I was driving through the fields like I normally do to check on all my babies. There's a cluster of trees in the southwest corner of the property that is near the woods that connect our property to the next county. I always call it no man's land. We hardly ever go out there. I don't like having the horses so far way. Normally we just use that area for hay, but I thought I'd see how the grass was doing so I was just going to drive by on my way back to the barn.

"I thought I saw a person there and figured it was one of our boys checking fence lines or maybe hiding from doing some work. I thought I'd go see which one it was.

"I parked the car and went through a cluster of trees until I came upon a clearing."

Marshall heard her breathing quicken and the slight raise in her voice. Whatever happened to Mrs. Wyatt, happened out there in the woods.

"It was horrible! Absolutely horrible. There were stacks and stacks of wire cages and these dogs were crammed into them. They were barking and a dead cat was hanging from the tree right in front of the dogs. There was blood and some of the dogs looked severely injured. I was going to get a closer look so I could tell Katelyn what I had found, but then I was hit on the back of the head. I fell to the ground. My bell was quite rung, but I managed to hear someone run away."

"Do you know which way he ran?" Marshall had taken his notepad out the second she started recounting her story.

"Deeper into the woods. I got up as soon as everything stopped spinning and came right here." Mrs. Wyatt paused and then looked to her husband, "Beauford, there were all these poor dogs. We have to go back and get them."

"Wait a second. Why don't you just tell me where this place is and I'll go there and check it out. I want to secure the scene."

"Pish posh. Beauford, get your gun. Katelyn, grab your medical bag. We're going to go rescue those poor dogs."

"No, ya'll stay here. I'll…" Marshall tried to tell a very determined looking Mrs. Wyatt.

"Son, you need to learn when you're in a no-win fight and just surrender. It saves a lot of time," Beauford said as he turned to a large gun case behind his mahogany desk and pulled out an antique Winchester 30-30 rifle. "Come on Sweet Pea, lead the way."

Marshall climbed into his cruiser and waited. The town had to be satisfied with its gossip and Mrs. Wyatt was happily giving it to them. He looked out the rearview mirror at her. She looked like an avenging angel in that white dress of hers and matching wide brimmed hat. He could see her hands gesturing in the air and, by the look on their faces, that she held them captive by her story. She had reached the part about being on her way to rescue the dogs.

Finally Beauford gently cut her off and maneuvered her to the Town Car. Even from where he was, Marshall could hear Beauford ordering the troops to go back to town and let the sheriff do his job. No wonder this man was feared in the boardroom. He looked like he came from one of those Civil War paintings Mrs. Wyatt had hanging up, except instead of having on a uniform he had a suit.

He watched as Beauford opened the door and helped Mrs. Wyatt into the car. He then reached back and grabbed the large medical bag Katelyn held and put it into the backseat. Marshall had wanted to give Katelyn a hard time about the attempted burglary at the clinic last night and to find out where she really stood with Ahmed, but Mr. and Mrs. Wyatt hadn't given him a chance to talk privately to her.

He liked Ahmed, but the thought of him with Katelyn turned his stomach. Something primal from deep inside him reared its head screaming that she was his. The trouble was that if she and Ahmed were together, as much as he hated it, he would have to deal with it. If he didn't, friend or not, Ahmed could find a way to make him disappear.

Marshall followed the pink Town Car through the fields and to the back of the property. He pulled up alongside Beauford when he slowed to a stop in front of the beginning of the woods.

"Ruthie says it was just through there." Beauford gestured to the trees.

"Okay. Keep them here. I'll check it out and then come back for you when I have secured the area."

At Beauford's nod he drove on ahead until the woods prevented his passage. As he got out on foot, he didn't know what to expect. Between the fighting dog Ahmed found and the description Mrs. Wyatt gave, he was afraid there was a dog-fighting ring in or near Keeneston.

He stopped and listened to the woods. Leaves rustled with the light breeze. Birds chirped and the sun danced through the trees. It didn't seem to be an area infested with the likes of dog fighting.

He looked around and through the trees saw the beginning of the clearing Mrs. Wyatt had told him about. As he broke through the tree line he knew with one look his fears of a dog-fighting ring were valid.

Blood was spattered around a makeshift wooden ring. Chains were piled up in a corner. He could see where the cages had been placed in the grass by the indents, but they were gone now. A dead cat was dangling from a tree branch.

He spun around with his gun drawn when he heard a noise come from behind him. Katelyn stood with her medical bag in one hand and her other hand covering her mouth. Her eyes were wide as she looked in horror at the carnage left behind. Bloody feathers covered the one side of the clearing. Farther back, tucked behind some trees, Marshall spotted the bodies of several dead dogs. He glanced back at Katelyn and saw the tears trickling down her cheeks.

"Sweet Lord," Beauford mumbled.

"What kind of monster could do such a thing, Beauford?" Mrs. Wyatt asked as she clutched her husband's arm.

"I don't know Sweet Pea, I just don't know. But, what I do know is there is a special place in Hell for them." He patted her hand and looked sadly upon the clearing.

Marshall was about to tell them to go back to their cars when a noise reached his ears. He wasn't the only one to hear it. Everyone had gone quiet and stared at a rustling bush nearby. Marshall held up his hand and signaled Beauford. Beauford stepped in front of his wife and leveled his 30-30 at the bush as Marshall drew his own 9mm Glock.

Katelyn watched as Marshall took his gun from his holster and pointed it at the moving bush. She was holding her breath, waiting to see who was there.

"Keeneston Sheriff. Come out slowly with your hands up," Marshall said loudly and clearly. "Katelyn, get behind me," he whispered.

Katelyn rolled her eyes, but with the memory of the other night fresh in her mind and no pooper-scooper in sight, she grudgingly stepped behind his wide shoulders. A sudden memory to four months ago flashed through her mind. His voice repeating his order to come out brought her back to the now.

The bush moved again and Marshall slowly inched forward. He held the gun in his right hand and with his left he slowly moved a branch out of the way. She watched him as he looked down toward the ground.

"Damn!" He quickly holstered his gun and fell to his knees.

Katelyn tightened her hand on her medical bag, but couldn't see over Marshall. She stepped forward and gasped at the vision she saw over Marshall's shoulder.

"What is it, darlin'?" Beauford asked as he started forward.

Katelyn was too busy to answer. She pushed Marshall out of the way and went to her knees beside the injured dog. She opened her medical bag and grabbed the saline wash and a bunch of gauze.

The dog before her was black, about forty pounds, and female. There was too much blood to tell much else. She checked the dog's pulse and found it weak. Her gums were white with lack of oxygen and her eyes were glazed. She wet the gauze and started her exam. There were bites on the neck, ears, and hind legs. Blood was flowing freely and she needed to operate to save her life, and quickly.

"Lord have mercy," her grandfather whispered.

Katelyn wrapped a tight layer of gauze around the biggest wounds on the dog's neck and leg. She slowly flipped her over and saw the massive tears down her side.

"Here." She shoved the gauze into Marshall's hand. "Wrap that around her as best and tight as you can. Then we need to get her into your cruiser and get to the house as fast as we can. Sorry Nana, I'll need your kitchen table. I need to operate and close these wounds before she bleeds out. Papa, I need you to call all your farm workers and have anyone with a large or medium sized dog come to the house immediately to donate blood."

"I'll buy you a new table, Sweet Pea."

Her grandmother shot daggers at him. "As if I care about a stupid kitchen table. Just go and save that precious little dog."

Katelyn used every suture and every drop of local anesthetic she had. The dog had lost half of one ear and there would be a nasty scar that ran the length of the side of her neck. But, she was alive and awake.

What surprised her more than the dog actually living was the fact that the dog showed no aggression. Most fighting dogs took months of rehabilitation and training to learn how to be loved and to give love. This little girl was just full of it. She was tentative, but so very sweet.

"Well, I think that does it. I'll take her to the clinic tomorrow morning. All she'll need is to be monitored, have her wounds cleaned, and then the stitches removed in ten days. She'll probably be fit for adoption after a round of antibiotics."

"I'm sorry, darlin', but I'm afraid I can't let you do that."

"Why not Papa?" She was tired and hurting. The last thing she wanted was to argue with her grandfather. But she didn't understand why he wouldn't let her treat this little dog.

"This sweet little thing is staying right here with me. I talked it over with your Nana, and we've agreed. Katelyn, meet Alice!"

Katelyn looked over to her grandmother who had tears in her eyes and to her grandfather, whose eyes were similarly misty and then to Alice who managed to find the strength to thump her tail and give her grandfather's hand a lick.

She was so happy she felt her eyes tear up. Her grandparents would give Alice all the love she needed to get over the trauma that happened to her. At the sound of Marshall clearing his throat she turned around to find him right behind her and looking very serious.

"Katelyn. I'm glad she's alright and even happier she has a good family now, but I need to talk to you...now."

Chapter Five

Marshall led the way out of the room and into the sitting room at the front of the house. Katelyn watched as he went over to the unlit fireplace and looked up at the antique rifle hanging on the wall.

"We have a problem," he said seriously to the rifle, but she was pretty sure it was meant for her.

"Duh just doesn't seem intellectual enough for me to say, but, duh." A problem with flashbacks to him naked in bed, her leaping behind cars to hide from him, and don't forget going hungry because he was always at the Café.

Marshall fought the urge to roll his eyes, it made him feel like such a girl. Instead he clenched his jaw and counted to ten as he watched her put her hands on her hips and stare him down. She had been amazing so far with Alice. Her long blonde hair had been pulled back into a tight ponytail and sheer determination had set on her face.

Her normally bright blue eyes turned navy as she focused on saving Alice. When he looked at her he saw a beautiful and intelligent woman. Not the dumb blonde model he normally saw. Why? Why did he have to be so damn attracted to the one woman who drove him so nuts?

"Between what I saw tonight and the information your boyfriend gave me the other night about the dog he found," he paused. He hoped she'd deny it, but she kept her face void of expression and didn't say a word. There's that ice princess he'd always known. "There's no reason to act in theory anymore. There's an obvious dog-fighting ring in my county, or at least around my county."

"It would seem so. Although, I'm not surprised. How much do you know about dog fighting, Sheriff?"

He ground his teeth together and blew out an agitated breath. Was she always so cold and indifferent? "Marshall. Call me Marshall. I think after sleeping together we can call each other by our first names, even if you were a coward and snuck out before breakfast."

Ah-ha! He finally got a reaction this time. Her eyes flashed with anger, a flush crept up her neck, and he smiled and rocked back on his heels when she shot him a look that would scare most men.

"As I was saying, Sheriff, I've seen all different levels of dog fighting in my life. Before I made a name for myself as a model, I had to do some more extreme shoots to get known. One of the shots was this editorial about gangs and I was posed in the middle of South Chicago. Young men would use dogs and dog fighting as a way to climb the gang ladder. The more fearsome the dog, the more status the owner got."

"So, it's just a status symbol?"

"On that level, yes. Then there's the polar opposite. The ones with money. They are the professionals. That's the highest level of fighting. It's extremely organized and extremely dangerous. They hire out poor and struggling models for more than modeling. They call them hostesses, but I don't even know if you could call them prostitutes. My roommate was hired as a server for one of these and when she came back she had nightmares for months. She had been groped and assaulted, witnessed drug and weapons trading and then actually saw a night of dog fighting. She had to go to therapy."

"It's that bad?"

"On that level, yes. It's ruthless. But, this reminds me more of what I saw when I was at veterinarian school in Auburn. They're kind of in the middle of the levels. They are way more organized and have more money than the gangs, but they don't have as much as the professionals. They are usually regional as opposed to international, like the professionals are. So, this ring here could be made up of fighters from Keeneston and the surrounding counties."

"I just don't get it. I have never thought of killing a dog as a means of status. I've seen a lot of things during wartime, but most of my men saved dogs. They certainly didn't kill them for sport or popularity." Marshall remembered several of his men giving what little food they had on them to dogs who would follow them as they trekked across the mountains.

"These bastards see their dogs as warriors, gladiators who, with every win, increase their standing in the community. But, the more realistic reason is money. Gambling is huge at every level of fighting. Winners can win big, from a couple hundred dollars to a couple hundred thousand dollars."

Marshall thought about it for a minute. This gave him a really good place to start. Katelyn had been helpful and he had been an ass to embarrass her about their night together. It just really irritated him that it seemed to mean more to him than to her. But, he should apologize and they should talk about that night. They needed to clear the air.

"Thank you. That gives me a place to start the investigation. Look, Katelyn, I also wanted to talk to you alone so that we…"

"Katelyn, dear, this nice young man came to check on me and then asked about you."

Marshall watched as Mrs. Wyatt walked through the door. Who was this nice young man? The second his black polished loafer came through the door, Marshall knew who it was. Son of a… he balled his hands into fists and narrowed his eyes.

"Ahmed."

"Marshall."

He watched as Ahmed came into the room and his eyes similarly narrowed. So, it must be true. Katelyn was dating Ahmed.

"Hello, Ahmed. It's so nice of you to come check on us."

"Anytime. It is my pleasure."

Crap. Ahmed smiled, he actually smiled. He was playing dirty. Marshall knew he had lost when a silly little smile came across Katelyn's face and for a minute she didn't look like the ice princess he was used to.

"I'm sorry, what where you going to say, Sheriff?" The silly smile left her face as she turned to him.

"Nothing. It's not important. Goodbye."

He walked out of the room with anger boiling in his stomach. Good riddance. It wasn't like he was competing for her or anything. He didn't want a snobby silver spoon ice princess. Even as he told himself that, there was a part of him that knew he was lying.

Katelyn turned from where she had watched Marshall stalk out the door. That man infuriated her more than any other man she knew, and that was saying a lot. Ahmed was still standing near her and she felt his strength radiating off of him. He had smiled at her and she had gone goofy for a minute.

He was a handsome man in a dark and mysterious sort of way. His black hair was cut straight across the nape of his neck. It was a little longer on top, which he kept slicked back. He had a perpetual five o'clock shadow that made him simultaneously sexier and more dangerous.

His black suit was impeccable. Under that black suit, he was thick and strong in a way you develop from working hard your whole life. But, that smile is what melted her. His normally tight lips and serious face transformed in those few seconds he smiled at her. For those brief seconds, he looked soft and caring.

Here was a man the total opposite of Marshall. He was trustworthy, loyal, secure, and he obviously cared about her and her family. This was the type of man she needed to be thinking about, not Marshall.

"How are you doing? Your grandmother told me about you saving little Alice." His smooth voice enveloped her as he moved toward her.

"Tired. And worried about all the dogs we didn't save. Nana said there were lots of them."

"I want you to take some of my men. I worry about you and your family. My men will keep you safe."

Katelyn moved over to the couch and sat down. She gestured for him to have a seat and felt the cushion dip as he sat down, bringing her slightly closer to him.

"I'm more worried about these dogs than I am about myself. The place was so bad, Ahmed. There was so much blood. What those poor dogs went through."

"I know. In my life I have seen many such fights unfortunately."

"You have?" she asked, surprised someone so sensitive to dogs would ever be present at such a violent event.

"Yes. I was hunting down a brutal man named Sergei and discovered the world of dog fighting. I never found him, but unfortunately I had to learn about this world he is a part of.

"There is a group of men and some women that fight these dogs on a large, international level. These fights are hard to find, but if you have the right contacts you can get in. I have had to find them before because of the other dealings that go on at fights. The weapons' trade mostly. It is horrific what they do. They would never think of fighting to the death themselves, but it is okay for them to do it to an animal. Cowards are what they are. Cowards who think they are gods."

"There's so much more to you, isn't there?"

"There's only one way to find out," he said as his voice lowered seductively. "There is?"

"Come to dinner with me."

Katelyn felt the catch in her breath. Dinner with Ahmed? Yes, please!

"I'd love to. But I also need to check on Zoti." Did her voice sound breathy?

"Perfect. I'd like to see him too."

"Let me just go tell Nana that I won't be here for dinner. I'll meet you out front?"

"I'll go get the car." And then he smiled again.

It took her a couple of minutes to realize he had left the room already. She shook her head and walked out through the door and down the hallway toward her grandfather's office.

"Yes! You heard right." Nana's voice floated into the hallway. "She's going on a date with him!"

Katelyn hurried into the office and found her grandpa on the couch with Alice wrapped in a blanket on his lap, sound asleep.

"I know! I can't believe it either."

She looked around the room and saw Nana standing at a side table with the phone to her ear.

"Nana!"

"Gotta go, Lily. We'll talk more later." She hung up the phone and turned innocently around. "Yes, dear?"

"As if you didn't already know, Ahmed and I are going out to dinner tonight."

"That's lovely, dear. Have a good time." Her grandmother smiled serenely as if she didn't just get caught gossiping.

"Call me if Alice needs me."

Her grandfather just nodded and went back to petting Alice's head. She was sure the second she left the house her grandmother would be back on the phone telling the whole town her granddaughter finally had a date.

Ahmed was waiting beside a brand new black Mercedes SUV with the passenger door open. The setting sun cast a warm glow about Ahmed as she walked towards him. She hadn't been on a date for almost two years. She had simply been too busy with wrapping up school and starting her own clinic.

"Are you ready?" he asked.

"Yes. I believe I'm finally ready," she smiled as she got into the car.

Katelyn took the stethoscope out of her ears and smiled. Ahmed was watching her closely as she finished up the exam on Zoticus. She and the rest of the girls had been calling him Zoti. It had taken a lot of work on their behalf, but he was starting to realize he wasn't in danger anymore. He didn't growl when they came to the run to feed him or give him his medicine. In fact, he had even allowed them to pet him.

Zoti wagged his tail just a little when she patted him on his hip before standing up to put away her instruments.

"He looks really good. I believe he's going to make it. I gave him some more antibiotics and a little more pain medication. He should be able to go home soon. Do you know what you're going to do with him?"

"Zoticus's new home is all ready for him. I bought a nice dog bed until he's strong enough to jump up onto the bed and couch. I have already hired a personal trainer to help me train him and to help him get over the memories I know he will suffer from. In time, I hope for him to be a normal, happy, and loved dog that will enjoy the rest of his life."

Katelyn's heart warmed as she watched Ahmed slowly pet Zoti's head. The dog looked up at Ahmed adoringly. In the dog's mind this man was his savior and she bet Zoti would spend the rest of his life thanking Ahmed for it.

He was nothing like Marshall. Even with their dogs. Bob had that same cocky, I know more than you do, attitude his owner had. No, Ahmed was better for her than Marshall. So, she needed to stop thinking of him and focus on what was right in front of her.

She needed a secure man in her life. After the example of her mother, she quite feared anything else. Her mom had a thing for rich assholes like her father and the six or so men after him. She had watched her mom depend on these men day after day until she was shipped off to boarding school at the request of one of them that didn't want a little brat hanging around.

Her mom didn't want to work and the men she was with didn't want her to. Her identity was to be solely wrapped up in them. She'd go wherever they wanted, do whatever they wanted, all to make sure she had as much money to spend as she wanted on clothes and a fancy car to drive.

Even at seven years old she knew it was wrong. She wanted to be known for who she was, not as a trophy girlfriend to be discarded the second she became blemished or the man got bored. So she worked hard at school. Her father was too busy running his empire to "get away" and see her at boarding school. Her mother was the same way. She was always too busy with her latest husband to visit her daughter. But, every holiday or break, a plane ticket always arrived from her grandparents with a note begging her to join them.

Then during her senior year of high school her father showed up. She hadn't seen him for three years. A bit of her heart leapt at the chance to show him what a good girl she was and to finally get approval. However, it was not to be. He arrived in pomp and circumstance. Bodyguards secured the area and ordered the principal of the school around as if she were a servant. It was all just part of the show. The real show was offering his daughter the chance to go to Yale—he had already secured her a spot—and intern with Jacks Hotels during the summers.

She had thought it wonderful until he told her it was because he was trying to take over a company that was family run and they didn't want to sell to someone as cold hearted as he. So, he came to collect his ignored daughter and play father until the deal closed in two or three years. He was going to go in as minority owner and it would take him that long to win them over and out of the remainder of control.

With a broken heart she turned him down, and he threatened to cut her off when she turned eighteen. She cried as he left and knew it would be the last time she'd let someone have power over her. She decided to strike out on her own. When she turned eighteen she signed a contract with a small modeling agency for one year. It was barely enough to pay the rent. She luckily received a scholarship and attended Barnard College in New York City so she could pursue her modeling career at the same time.

She lived with some of her friends from the boarding school nearby. At the end of her first year she had almost failed out. With the pressures of modeling, she fell behind in the rough liberal arts' curriculum. The teachers worked with her and she scored high enough to stay in school, but on academic probation.

That summer when her contract was up she signed with the premier modeling agency and started booking major shows. She worked every day during the summer. There was no more time to go see her grandparents. She was walking the runways in Milan, doing photo shoots for Victoria's Secret, Versace, and Ralph Lauren. Money was rolling in and she took a semester off school to continue modeling. She did manage to take online courses.

She moved into her own small apartment and saved every penny she could. She worked hard and constantly for two more years before taking time off and going back to school with photo shoots scheduled around her school schedule. By then, she had enough online credits to be a junior. Katelyn finished up school, nearly making honors in spite of the rough start, and applied for veterinary school. She had always loved the animals at her grandparents' farm and felt the calling. She had decided to go to Auburn. It was a good school and far away from the New York craziness.

Her agency had struck a deal with her. They'd only book shoots and runways around her school schedule. It turned out the more unavailable you were, the more designers wanted you. She was able to work her way through graduate school while enjoying the times she went on shoots because they weren't constant. She had lost her scholarship after the first semester at Barnard, but had made enough to pay her tuition for the online courses and to pay full tuition when she went back full time. She even had enough to pay for graduate school. She was free of debt when she graduated and that allowed her to focus on the next phase of her life.

After Katelyn graduated from Auburn, she knew she was getting too old to model and she now had what she wanted, a real career. She was a doctor and she wanted to start her own clinic. She left the modeling world while on top and came back to the only home she had ever known, only to mess up the peace by sleeping with Marshall.

But now she had a chance to correct that mistake... that hot, passionate mistake. Ahmed was here and he was doing everything right. An actual date! "A tough man with a soft side" she thought as she watched him pet and talk to Zoti.

"Thank you for such a wonderful dinner. How did you find that place?" Katelyn asked as Ahmed led her toward her door.

"I like to know all the places around town. The good, bad, and ugly."

"Well, this was definitely ugly, but it was the best catfish I've ever had," she laughed about the restaurant, which would be better described as a hole in the wall.

They had a wonderful time. Ahmed told her of the beaches and scenery of his home country of Rhami. They didn't talk about family though. She didn't want to talk about her parents and she had a feeling he didn't want to talk to about his either. He was kind, attentive, and everything a date should be.

"I had a nice time," Ahmed slipped his hand into hers and walked her up the stairs.

"I did too. Thank you so much for a wonderful dinner."

"I would like to do it again, if you're free."

"That would be great. I'd love to." Katelyn's heart sped up as Ahmed raised her hand to his lips.

"Goodnight, Katelyn."

"Goodnight." She watched as he walked back to his car and got in.

She turned the doorknob and tried to open the door. It stopped short and she heard a thump as if something fell to the ground. Katelyn put her eye to the crack in the door and saw her grandmother flat on her bottom.

"Nana! Were you eavesdropping?"

"Me?" she asked innocently.

"Is that a cell phone in your hand?"

"Oh, um, I'll get the recipe to you first thing in the morning. Goodnight Lily." Then her grandmother had the audacity to smile at her and shrug her shoulders. Great, she could hear the phones ringing all around town.

Chapter Six

Marshall stabbed the last bite of his lunch at the Blossom Café. As if he wasn't agitated enough with having a dog-fighting ring in town, he now had to spend his lunch listening all about the date of the century.

"Then he raised her hand to his lips and kissed it!" Miss Daisy twittered to a table full of women.

He cringed as he heard the chorus of sighs. The second he set foot in the café he couldn't go a second without hearing every single detail of the date. How long they were gone, where they had gone to dinner, how Ahmed was so gentlemanly, and about that damned kiss. For crying out loud, it wasn't even a real kiss! It was nothing like the ones he and Katelyn shared that night. He slammed his fork down on his plate and tossed some money on the counter before stalking out of the café.

He had something better to do. He had an investigation to run. He had started this morning with some research and was waiting to hear from Sheriff Nuggett from Lipston County. With the activities taking place so close to the county line, he thought it was best to bring in the neighboring law enforcement to make sure there were no gaps in information between the two offices.

The door to the café closed on some more sighs, which caused him to close his eyes and count to ten for patience. Who cared what

Katelyn Jacks did? He had never been so happy to hear his radio go off.

"Hey Marsh, Sheriff Nuggett is in your office. He got your message and wanted to meet in person," Annie's voice told him.

"I'm just across the street, I'll be right there."

"Sheriff Davies, it's nice to finally meet you."

"It's nice to meet you too. Thanks for coming all the way out here to talk to me."

Marshall shook the sheriff's hand and sat down behind his desk. Sheriff Nuggett was what you'd call a good ol' boy. He was in his mid-forties, had brown hair cut short and looked like he was either retired military or some kind of sports player. He was muscular, but had started to soften with age. He wore a smile and was generally relaxed as he took a seat.

"Military or sports?" Marshall asked.

"Both. Kentucky National Guard and football. I'm guessing you were military."

"Ranger." They smiled and Marshall knew they'd be able to work well together. "Where'd you play ball?"

"Western Kentucky."

"In your time there, did you ever figure out what exactly Big Red the Hilltopper was?"

"No, but he was a very energetic mascot." Nuggett laughed. Turning serious he pulled out a notepad and flipped it open. "Tell me about this dog-fighting ring."

Marshall shared info about the dog Ahmed found and the assault on Mrs. Wyatt. He described the horrible sight they came upon in the clearing and watched as Nuggett scribbled on the notepad.

"Did the little dog live?"

"Yes, Katelyn did save the dog."

"Thank goodness. Well, what you're describing sounds a lot like experiences I've been having in my county. A couple of boys came upon a site a lot like you described, but there were no animals found.

Just some blood and the grass trampled down around the whole area."

"What do you think of a joint task force between our departments?" Marshall asked.

"I think it's the only way to cover the area. My guess is they are hosting these fights on the county lines in hopes of us not knowing what's going on next door, so to say. If we combine resources, then we'll have the whole picture and not just a partial one."

"I've started looking at people with violent charges and charges against animals in my county already," Marshall told him as he pulled out a stack of papers.

"I think it's also a good idea to get a map together of where all the known fights took place and then highlight the areas that are similar in hopes of catching them."

"I'll put that together and email it to you so you can put it on your map."

"I'll do the same. It's been nice to meet you Davies. Hopefully we can get these guys before they have another fight."

"I hope so too."

Marshall watched Nuggett leave and went straight to work on the map. If they could narrow down the areas, he could patrol them, hopefully stop a fight before it happened, and arrest all the participants. And, with any luck, diving into the investigation would drive a certain blonde out of his mind for a while.

Camille Watkins pushed the end button on her cell phone and smiled. She had been riding one heck of a lucky streak recently. Two of their dogs were close to champion status. With their breeding program up and running and the success of the regional Warrior's Association, they finally had enough money to buy a large farm of their own to expand their fighting dog kennel named Gladiator.

"Yo, Andre!" She screamed down the hall of their three-bedroom house they had bought a couple years ago.

She worked as a secretary at a medical office and Andre was an independent contractor. He was able to keep his schedule flexible so he could train their dogs. It worked out perfectly. They had started training dogs almost ten years ago. They met in high school and moved to Georgia right after they got married. That's where they fell in love with the sport of dog fighting. The glamour of the competition, the drama of the action in the ring. It was exhilarating. After a minor incident in Georgia, they moved up to Kentucky with Andre's brother and quickly rose to the top ranks of dog fighting. Now was their time to shine.

"I'm in the basement, babe."

Camille walked to the kitchen and stirred the spaghetti sauce she had simmering for dinner before heading downstairs. The basement spanned the whole length of their brick ranch home. She was proud of her home, but even prouder of their kennel. Her husband looked up from where he was training their youngest puppy as she reached the bottom of the stairs.

"Did Crow kill that cat by himself?"

"Sure did. I tossed the cat into his kennel. He's a good pup."

She could see her husband's pride as he watched Crow. The pup had just turned eight months old and her husband had started his more aggressive training a couple of months ago. This was his first solo kill and she knew Andre would be ecstatic.

"I heard from our contact. The reports that were given to International on us were good. Luckily the scout left town right after the fight and didn't see the issue with cleanup."

"That is good news. That old woman came out of nowhere, but I gave us enough time to get all the dogs home." Andre stood up and wiped his hands on his gray t-shirt.

"Well, there's more news." Camille tried not to bounce up and down with excitement.

"Did International accept our application already?"

"No, not yet. However, the report from whoever saw the fight was enough to get us on the radar. Sometime in the next couple of fights a member of the International Warrior's Association will come and meet with us in person! We're almost there, honey! We're so close!" Andre lifted up his wife and swung her around with a yell.

"How much cash do we have on hand and how much can we get? We need our next fights to be big time." Andre paced as he waited for his wife to calculate the money.

"We have ten grand on hand and with proper marketing and listing online on the forum I'm sure we can get some sponsors to have the winner get $25,000 in prize money."

"Let's do it, babe! Call our contacts and make sure we find a time when the law is occupied. We also need to find a new place. That place on the farm worked so well until that old lady stumbled upon it." Andre gave his wife a kiss and patted her bottom to hurry her up the stairs.

"I know. It had such good access from all the counties. I'll look around and try a new place to throw the cops off. I'll let you know what I find and then we can go check it out."

"Sounds like a plan, babe. Check with our contacts when you call them and see if they have any locations in mind too. Mmm, dinner smells great."

"Thanks, hon."

Yes indeed, things were going good for them and on Sunday she'd thank God for it during prayer at church.

Katelyn gave Zoti a pat on his head and was rewarded with a little tail wag. All the people in the clinic had been working hard to train him over the past couple of days. Since the night of her date with Ahmed, she knew Zoti would be going home soon. And now, three days later, he was ready to go.

"You look good, boy. You can go home with your new daddy." She looked up to a beaming Ahmed and smiled. "You take good care of him. Give him lots of rest and encouragement. He'll need training soon to help him adjust to his new life. Along with training, lots of love will help heal the wounds of abuse." Katelyn placed her hand in Ahmed's outstretched one and let him help pull her up from the ground.

"I can do all of that. I bought him food, bowls, a collar, leash, and multiple beds for the house."

Katelyn reached down and placed her hand on Zoti's big, wide head. Ahmed's warm dark hand reached for Zoti's head at the same time. His fingers intertwined with hers and she knew he was going to kiss her. She wanted this so badly. In her dreams he'd sweep her off her feet and kiss her with such passion that she couldn't help but fall in love.

Ahmed pulled her close and she felt her body go willingly. She placed her hand on his chest and felt nothing but raw strength. Zoti and Ahmed weren't all that different. She looked up into his eyes. They were black with passion as he brought his hand up to cup her cheek.

She felt his thumb caress her softly. Her stomach was doing flips and she watched in almost a state of disbelief as he brought his lips toward hers. It was a slow, deep kiss and the passion was... not there.

Katelyn pulled back and looked into Ahmed's face to see if she could read it. His face was blank and then he smiled again. Under her hand she felt him start to laugh quietly.

"Why are you laughing?"

"Your face is priceless. I can see the worry all over it. Don't worry. I didn't feel it either." Ahmed's smile dropped and for the first time since she'd been in Keeneston she saw sadness in his eyes.

"I wanted it to work. I wanted it to work so badly," she sighed and squeezed his hand.

"I know. Maybe a man like me, a man who has done the things I have, doesn't deserve to find love."

"Ahmed…"

"No, don't pity me. You're really not good at hiding what you're thinking Katelyn. I'm so thankful that you gave it a chance—a lot of women wouldn't have. But, I am hoping for one more thing from you."

"Of course, anything."

"I want your friendship. You are a wonderful person and I'm lucky to have you as a friend."

Katelyn felt her heart break. She had wanted that passion, that spark, to be there. It just hadn't been. It felt, well, it felt just as if she was kissing her friend.

"Of course!"

"Good. Thank you for saving Zoti." Ahmed leaned forward and kissed her cheek. When she opened her eyes he and Zoti were heading out of the room.

Dammit. She didn't know what bothered her most. That the spark wasn't there or when she had closed her eyes and kissed Ahmed, she had thought of a certain hazel-eyed sheriff. God, could things get any worse?

Marshall tried to smile at the woman across from him at his mother's dinner table. Pierce was on one side of him humming the bridal march under his breath and Miles was on the other side doing his best to talk to Cole the whole time.

Their mother had ambushed both he and his brother with two sisters she met at her hair salon. They had thought they were coming over for a quick dinner and instead came face to face with Prissy and Sissy. As her mother informed them during introductions, the girls were talented with hair and both wanted to be married and have kids soon.

Miles and Marshall had looked at each other with utter looks of fear and even Paige had tried to think of a reason for them to have to leave, but their mother had refused all attempts at escape.

"Is that your phone, Marshall? I thought I said no cell phones at the table," his mother gently chastised.

"Sorry, Ma, it's the office. They wouldn't have called if it wasn't an emergency."

"Well, at least tell Annie that she and Cade are expected here after her shift ends. You work her too hard."

"Yes, Ma." He answered the phone and talked to Annie before pushing his chair back in haste. "They're armed? I'll be right there." He hung up the phone and looked at the roomful of people staring at him. "Sorry, there's an emergency at the café. I have to go."

"Do you need my help?" Miles asked with a hint of hope in his voice.

"No, he surly doesn't," his mom answered for him. "Just hurry back before you boys head out for your poker night."

"Yes, Ma. Thanks for dinner, it was wonderful as always."

He kissed his mother's cheek and gave Miles a slap on the back as he hurried to the cruiser. He was going to need the lights for this one.

As Marshall approached the Blossom Café a growing crowd prevented him from seeing the situation inside. He flashed his lights and pulled up to the curb.

"Sheriff! I'm glad you *finally* decided to show up. Is there so much crime in Keeneston that it takes you ten minutes to get to the scene of an assault?"

Marshall stopped the curse coming from his lips, but just barely. Standing in front of him in all his pompous glory was Jack Jacks. His sandy blonde hair sliced down the side of his head and folded perfectly into shape. He wore a dove gray suit and red power tie against a white shirt. And right now he was pissed.

Behind him was a white-haired army. Miss Daisy stood with a wooden spoon, Miss Violet with a spatula, and Miss Lily was armed with her broom. Most of the patrons had emptied out of the Café and were standing on the street watching the spectacle and most likely placing bets.

"Miss Daisy, what's going on here?"

"Why are you asking her? I told you I was assaulted and I want those women arrested and I want them arrested now!"

"Mr. Jacks, you may be used to ordering everyone around at your hotels but not here. So, be quiet and let me listen to her. You'll have your chance to speak." Marshall watched his tan face turn red in anger, but he stayed quiet.

"This man came in here and ordered me to close the whole café just so he could eat. He then said some very ungentlemanly things to me when I refused. He said he didn't want to eat with all the noise. It would disturb him. Then he got angry and started yelling. Well, I don't know how he was raised, but I don't take a shining to behavior like that in my place of business."

"So, what did you do?" Marshall could see Mr. Jacks demanding the place for himself. It was a typical move on his part.

"Well, I did as I would do to any of the boys in town, what I did to you when you back-talked me that one time when you were twelve." Uh-oh. Marshall knew what was coming next. "I rapped his knuckles with a wooden spoon," Miss Daisy said proudly.

"There, she admitted it. Arrest her!" Jacks shouted.

"Mr. Jacks, please be quiet. What happened next Miss Daisy?"

"Well, instead of taking the lesson that was being taught and apologizing for being rude, he leapt up and tried to yank the spoon away from me. That's when Violet called Lily and then she smacked his hand with the spatula."

Marshall stared at her with his eyes opening wider in surprise. He'd seen them do this routine to badly behaved kids trying to steal desserts, but never to an adult. Although, when he was around Mr. Jacks, he felt the urge to hit him too.

"Is that all?"

"No. Then I asked him to leave and he refused. That's when Lily came in and shooed him out with the broom."

"Is that everything?"

"Yes. But, I have to say this to him. Mr. Jacks, bless your heart, but you are one rude and entitled jerk." The town murmured their agreement, which only fueled Mr. Jack's temper.

"You crazy old bat. Maybe you and your sisters can get a job cooking in jail." Mr. Jacks shoved his hands into his pockets and rocked back on his heels, pleased with the idea of the Rose sisters in jail.

"Father! What in the hell do you think you're doing?"

Marshall watched as Katelyn pushed her way through the crowd. Her face was flushed and her body rigid.

"Cleaning up this town of no consequence. I'm glad to see you. I need to talk to you when I'm done having these three tossed into jail."

"Father. Stop it. You will do no such thing. You will apologize to all these people for being an ass right now."

"See Katie, you were always too soft. You need to let them know who's boss."

"Father, you are not their boss and they are not your employees. Now apologize right now and stop embarrassing me and yourself."

Her father paused and looked at the hostile crowd of people around him. Marshall watched as he debated what he wanted to do and he also watched the way Katelyn tried to hide her complete embarrassment.

"Fine. I'm sorry I yelled and even though you should be arrested, I'll let it go this time."

"He should've stopped after *I'm sorry*," Miss Daisy said to her sisters who all nodded in agreement.

"Okay. I'm sorry. Is that good enough?"

"Humph."

And with that the people of Keeneston turned and went back into the café leaving Mr. Jacks and his entourage on the sidewalk.

"I'm sorry for the trouble Sheriff," Katelyn said in a quiet voice. She was shy now, clearly upset at what had happened.

"It's alright. I should thank you for getting me out of a dinner at home."

Katelyn gave him a weak smile and ushered her dad into the big shiny black SUV waiting for him. Marshall looked down at his watch and smiled. Darn, too late for dessert at his mom's house. Too bad. Now it was time to play poker with the guys. But, he couldn't escape the bad feeling that he had jumped to some very wrong conclusions about Katelyn Jacks.

Chapter Seven

"I fold." Marshall laid his cards down and took a drink of his bourbon and coke. He was almost out of chips and it couldn't be soon enough. His mind was not in the game. He might as well just hand over his money.

"Marshall, ante up."

Cade nudged him and raised his eyebrow in question. Marshall tossed a chip into the center of the table and looked around Miles' new house as he waited for the bets to be placed. Miles had gone away from the traditional farmhouse that he, their parents, and Cade lived in, to a contemporary house with large windows overlooking the farm.

The house was extravagant in a totally understated way. It had large ceilings, two-story windows, and everything state of the art, shiny and new. It wasn't his style, but Miles had always been a little different from the rest of them. He liked suits and working in the corporate world. His house reflected it with sleek furniture and fancy artwork.

"Are you going to bet?" Cade asked him. "Or are you going to sit there staring off into space for the rest of the night?"

Marshall looked down at his cards. Nothing. Aw, what the heck.

"All in."

Twenty minutes later he sat down in a black leather chair and looked out over the fields as he sipped his drink. He saw Miles' reflection in the window and looked at his big brother.

"The house looks great Mi."

"Thanks. Now tell me what's going on."

"Just sitting here."

"You know that's not what I mean."

"Yeah, I know. Just thinking I made a mistake and I hate when I do that." Marshall looked down at the amber liquid in his glass and thought about Katelyn.

Miles clasped his shoulder and walked back to the poker table. Marshall's hand squeezed the tumbler as his thoughts turned to what Katelyn was doing now. She was probably with Ahmed, crying on his shoulder over her father's behavior. It should be his shoulder she was crying on. He downed the rest of his drink and reached for the decanter.

He had made a colossal mistake. He had been an ass for judging her on the basis of her father's actions. One of his first security assignments when he opened his own firm after he got out of the Army had been Jack Jacks. He had called and was coming into Lexington to ink a big deal for a new hotel.

The guy had been an entitled prick the whole time. He ordered people about constantly. He treated his assistants horribly. He berated them, ignored them, and yelled at them. To add insult to injury, he never once said thank you. It was just one demand after another.

Marshall had listened to him during his meeting about Katelyn, his hot shot model daughter, and just assumed she was as bad as her father. She had always been so quiet and cold when he saw her around town. But, he realized that was just his prejudice blinding him. He had mistaken shyness for coldness. He had mistaken her quietness for arrogance and snobbery.

What an idiot he had been. He had never even given her a chance. He should've known better. Any person who was so good and kind to animals couldn't be that cold and uncaring as he had previously thought. And any person who had made love to him the way she did couldn't be the snob he had thought.

But, now it was too late. He had lost his chance to really get to know her. If he hadn't been so blind, he could've been getting to know her over these last four, almost five months since their night together. Who knows where they'd be now. But it was all for nothing, she was with Ahmed now.

Katelyn couldn't be more exhausted. She had stayed up all night fighting with her father before he left on his private jet in the morning. She had never been so embarrassed. As she got dressed in her scrubs for work she was, for the first time, not looking forward to going. Her father had come in and disrupted the only place she knew as home and now she had to go face everyone. She had to face the fact that everyone would whisper about her father as they gave her pitying looks, or worse, judged her based on his actions.

"Katelyn!" She jumped as she heard her grandmother scream, in the most lady-like fashion as possible of course.

The tone of her grandmother's voice surprised her and she bolted down the stairs. She spotted her grandmother's hat first and then her laced gloves waving in the air. As she got farther down the stairs she saw that the person she was attacking with lace was the farm manager, Joey Heath.

Joey had his hat in his hand and was tapping it against his jean-clad leg as he and her grandmother stared out the door towards the front pasture. They talked quickly and Joey kept shaking his head. When he heard her near, he looked pleadingly at her for help.

"What's going on Nana?"

"Joey found something! Come on, you've got to see it." Nana adjusted her red wide-brimmed hat that matched her lipstick and headed out the door.

Her grandmother was in the lead and Joey followed dutifully behind toward a new section of fencing. Her grandmother stopped and looked down the hole where she guessed a fence post was supposed to go. Katelyn looked down and saw something black.

"What is it?" she asked.

"I don't know. It clanked when I hit it and that's when I came and got your grandmother. I didn't know what I should do," Joey told her.

"I think it's buried treasure." She hadn't seen her grandmother this excited in a long time. She couldn't stand still as she circled the hole.

"Nana, not everyone buries the family silver in the back yard like your family did."

"Does... it never stopped. It's kind of a family tradition ever since the war. Besides, it gives me an excuse to buy new flatware. All the women in the family do it when we're ready to redecorate. Joey, give me that shovel."

"Ma'am?"

"Well, you're not digging, so give it to me and I'll get it." She grabbed the shovel leaning against a newly planted fence post and shoved it into the ground near the black object.

Katelyn and Joey crowded around and watched as little by little more was revealed of the object. *Clank, Clank.* The noise filled the air and with a gasp Joey leapt forward and grabbed the shovel.

"Stop! That's not buried treasure, that's a freaking cannonball!"

"What?" Katelyn leaned forward and looked in the hole.

"I'm telling you, that's a cannonball." Joey stepped back and brought her grandmother with him.

"Well, you can't just leave it there. Dig it up and bring it into the house. Then I'll call Beauford and see what to do."

"Are you sure, ma'am?" Joey eyed the hole cautiously as if the cannonball may climb out on its own.

"I'm sure. If you don't want to do it, then just hand me that shovel back and I'll do it myself."

Katelyn stopped the snicker that was threatening to come out while she watched the wide brim of her grandmother's hat bounce as Nana placed her lace-gloved hands on her hips.

"Okay, Mrs. W, whatever you say."

Joey crept forward with the shovel and started to dig. Within a couple of minutes she watched as he carried the thick black ball into the house and put it on the kitchen table. Ruffles and her new best friend, Alice, came bounding over to check it out.

Ruffles had taken it upon herself to help nurse Alice back to health. The two had become almost inseparable this past week. Now the two of them were staring at the cannonball with the same look that Joey had.

"Beauford! Pick up the phone," her grandmother yelled into the phone.

"I don't think he can hear you, Nana."

"Well. I guess he'll be no help. Of course he chose today to go hunting with his buddies. Katelyn, dear, wasn't that nice young sheriff in the army? Give him a call and maybe he'll know what to do."

With a grimace Katelyn went to the phone. She had a decision to make. Well, who was she kidding, she was a coward. She called Annie and had her call Marshall.

Katelyn paced back and forth in front of the cannonball as she waited for the inevitable knock on the door. After yesterday and the way her father acted she didn't want to see Marshall. It was just one more reason he'd hate her.

At the sound of the doorbell she prepared herself for the worst. She straightened her back and put on the mask she wore to cover her insecurity. She could do this. But, when she saw him walk in, she felt a pain in her heart. Why was she so torn? She couldn't stand him, but longed for him at the same time. It was life's cruel joke on her.

He had the confidence she envied and the looks to back it up. His hazel eyes were sharp and his swagger was that of a real man, not some cocky wanna be. His eyes locked on hers and she tried to stare past him so she wouldn't see the pity or the hate. Hold on, he looked different. She actually looked at him now and saw that his eyes were soft and full of worry, not full of pity or cockiness.

"Are you alright? Is it your father?" He asked quietly.

"Oh, um, no. He left early this morning to see about a hotel in Hong Kong." She saw his brows crease as he looked around to make sure everyone was okay.

"Then, what is it?"

"Annie didn't tell you?"

"I guess she thought it would be more fun as a surprise," he said dryly with a wry smile coming across his face, emphasizing a small thin scar on his chin.

Katelyn couldn't help but return the smile. She stepped away from the kitchen table and held out her hands as if modeling a necklace on television. "Ta-da!"

"Is that a cannonball?"

"No, it's Nana's new hat. Isn't it lovely?" Katelyn deadpanned.

"It's lovely Mrs. Wyatt. Would you care to tell me about it?"

"Joey found it while digging a new fence post. We didn't know what to do with it. Where do you think it came from?" She watched as Marshall went over and put his arm around her grandmother.

"Too bad, it would've made you a lovely hat. Then again, everything looks lovely on you." He gave her a squeeze and a wink before heading over to the table to look at the cannonball.

She watched as he picked it up and turned it over. His eyes got big and he moved very slowly to put the old dented ball on the kitchen table. As soon as the ball was settled on the table he leapt backward. He grabbed Katelyn's arm with one hand and Mrs. Wyatt's hand with the other and simultaneously pulled them back to the doorway.

"Marshall, what are you doing?" Katelyn asked. She looked down where he was holding her hand and stared. His grip was strong, sure, and felt so warm.

"That cannonball is live. It's also very old and I don't know how stable it is."

"Live?" Katelyn took another step back.

"Yup. See that plug there? That means it's intact and live. The size, shape and condition make me think it's from the Civil War."

"There were no battles around here. Even I know that," Joey put in.

"True. But there were battles in Perryville and Richmond, which are pretty close to us. It's very possible there was a little skirmish and while the troops were moving this got left behind. That would explain why it's still live," Marshall told them.

"What do we do about it?" She wasn't too excited about the prospect of an almost 150-year-old cannonball being too near.

"We need to call Army Munitions." Marshall pulled out his cell phone and started searching for a phone number.

"What's the number? We can use the speaker phone." Her grandmother dialed the phone and everyone gathered around the phone to hear who answered.

"Army Munitions," an unidentified woman said.

"This is Captain Marshall Davies, Rangers, retired. I have a munitions question on a cannonball."

"One second Captain. I'll transfer you."

Katelyn looked around and tried not to laugh. Everyone was huddled around the phone staring at it eagerly. She had to admit, she had never seen Joey so worried before. She guessed the thought of her grandmother with a live cannonball was enough to finally get the normally unflappable manager completely flapped. Her grandmother on the other hand looked joyful. This was unexpected action and she loved every second of it.

Marshall though, was leaning against the wall next to the phone and looking completely bored. It was as if he was used to dealing with live ammunitions over a hundred years old on a daily basis. But, boy, did he look good being bored. She used the time to study his profile. He looked chiseled, like the statues she saw when she was modeling in Italy. His body was long and muscular. His uniform clung to those muscles, covering the nicest six-pack a girl had ever seen, and showed his tapered waist. His face had a strong jaw and sharp angles, but it was his eyes that had always fascinated her. She never knew which color they would be. Sometimes they were hazel, sometimes green, and sometimes brown. She also knew when he was in bed they turned a deep shade of brown and were filled with desire.

"This is Lieutenant Bell."

"Lieutenant, this is Captain Davies, retired. I'm the Sheriff in Keeneston, Kentucky. I have an interesting situation on my hands here and need your help."

"Sure thing Captain, what can I do for you?" he drawled. It appeared Lieutenant Bell was a good ol' southern boy.

"I'm going to let you talk to the person who found the cannonball, Mrs. Ruth Wyatt." Marshall stepped back and let her grandmother speak.

"Lieutenant Bell, you sound like you're from the great state of Georgia."

"Yes, ma'am. From Macon."

"I'm from Roswell, just outside of Atlanta myself."

"Well, you're from just up the road. Now, tell me about this cannonball."

Katelyn had a great time watching her grandmother retell the story. You'd think she was on stage instead of telling the story over the phone. Her hands flew, her face was animated and she moved around demonstrating how she used the shovel.

"What does the cannonball look like?"

"It's black. Smaller than a basketball," her grandmother answered.

"It's a nine pounder and the plug is still in it. I think it's from the Civil War," Marshall filled in.

"The plug is in it? Geez almighty. That thing is live! You need to talk to our historic munitions expert. Let me get his number. He's the only person in the Army who specializes in live munitions from that long ago. Here it is. I'll transfer you now."

"Thank you Lieutenant Bell." The line went quiet as the transfer was put through. "What a nice young man," her grandmother smiled and tapped her fingers against the table as she waited to be connected.

"Hello? Ma'am? Lieutenant Bell said you think you may have a live cannonball from the Civil War?" a voice said from over the phone.

"That's right," her grandma answered.

"Well, you don't see that every day. I will need to come to you to collect it and possibly detonate it if I have to."

"Really? Is it that big of a deal Mr..."

"Oh, I am sorry ma'am. It's Sargent Sherman, ma'am."

"I'm sorry, dear, did you say Sherman?"

Uh-oh. Katelyn knew that tone. Her grandmother rarely got angry, but this was her warning voice.

"Yes ma'am."

"Is there anyone else that can help me?"

"Um, no ma'am. I'm the only expert we have in Civil War munitions."

"I am so sorry Sergeant, but there has only ever been one Sherman on my property and there's never going to be another. Good day."

And with that, Katelyn watched as her grandmother hung up the phone and wiped her hands together before turning around and facing the open-mouthed group.

"Well then, I do believe this will make a lovely door stop. If it hasn't blown up in 150 years I doubt it'll blow up now." Mrs. Wyatt's lace-gloved hands picked up the cannonball and carried it away.

"Sherman? Really?" Marshall asked. His eyebrow shot up while his lips twitched.

"Well, he did burn her family farm."

"True. I should've known family honor never dies in the South. Even after 150 years," he snickered.

Marshall's radio buzzed and Annie's voice came over it, "Sheriff?"

"Excuse me for a minute." Marshall walked out to the sunroom behind the kitchen and talked into his radio for a minute. His head hung for a minute before he came back in to the kitchen.

"Your boyfriend found another dog on Mo's farm."

"Oh no. Is the dog alive?"

"I don't know. I'm sure Ahmed will call you soon." His voice was so tight now.

"I doubt it. While Ahmed is my friend, he's not my boyfriend."

"He's not? But everyone in town…"

"Is wrong. He's my friend, nothing more."

"Well, this is a first. I had never known the Keeneston gossip grapevine to be wrong. Do you want to grab your bag and come out to the farm with me?"

"Sure, I'll meet you at your car."

Katelyn ran up the stairs to her room and let the battle wage inside her head. He had seemed happy when he found out she wasn't dating Ahmed anymore. But, should she care? Probably not. It was probably just some macho mentality of his.

Marshall waited by the passenger door of the cruiser and wanted to do a happy dance. It made him feel foolish, so he just pumped his fist real fast when he was sure no one was watching him. He might still have a chance with her.

He turned when he heard the front door open and watched her come down the steps in her blue scrubs. He had never thought of scrubs as sexy, but he sure did now. He had to admit, she was beautiful when she was modeling, but she was amazing now. She has curves in all the right places. When he saw her, all he could think about was running his hands down those curves.

"You ready?" she asked.

"Yup. Here you go." He took her bag and opened the door for her. He needed to do things right this time.

Marshall parked the car and knew it wasn't a good outcome when he saw Dani crying in Mo's arms. He moved around the car and helped Katelyn over the uneven ground when he spotted Ahmed placing a blanket over a form on the ground.

"When you catch up to this SOB you better whoop his ass before you take him to jail," Katelyn murmured to him as they approached the figure.

Marshall thought the guy better pray Katelyn didn't find him first. He watched as she leaned down and pulled the blanket back. Dani started crying louder and buried her face in Mo's chest to hide her eyes from the view.

Katelyn released some very unpleasant words and he knew it had to be bad. He looked over her shoulder and gasped. He had never seen a body so mutilated. The poor dog must have suffered tremendously.

"What happened?"

"Dani and Mo were out riding and the horses suddenly started acting skittish. Dani almost got thrown, so they came back to the stables and got me. We all came out looking for the cause and found him lying here. I think he was heading for the small pond to get some water. The blood trail shows he came from the woods. There were ATV tracks there. He was probably dumped as dead. We would never have found him if he was actually dead. Those woods are thick and we never go in them." Ahmed pointed to where the dog had crawled out of the woods.

The leaves were green, the wildflowers brought beautiful color to the countryside, but now it was all marred by the image of the dog under the blanket.

"Did the tracks lead anywhere?"

"No. I lost them."

"Thanks for looking. Let me take some pictures and gather some evidence. Ahmed, can you show me the blood trail and the tracks you found in the woods?"

"Sure."

"Katelyn, can we take the dog back to your clinic and have you perform an autopsy for evidence?"

"Yes, that's fine." Katelyn had lost the spark in her eyes. Now, her lips were drawn tight and her arms folded over her chest. She was upset and, by the way she kept staring at the blanket and chewing on her lip, he suspected she was getting angry, very angry.

Marshall spent hours collecting evidence from the scene. Dinky helped him canvas the area as Noodle took the dog to the vet clinic. Mo, Dani, Ahmed, and Katelyn had stayed and watched, their heads together the whole time.

Marshall needed to revise the situation. He was sure any one of them would kill the person responsible. It also looked like they were plotting something. Southerners had their own brand of justice and he needed to make sure they remembered he was the law and he'd make sure this man, or men, got what they deserved.

"Okay, we're done here. It's a nice night out, let's go eat at the café and talk this over."

The night was pleasant so the group took a seat at the table in front of the café. The sun had almost set and the town was basking in the last orange rays before night fell. The days were becoming much longer now. It was almost nine at night, yet the sun was refusing to give way to the moon.

The café was mostly empty as closing time approached. The shops had closed and families were sitting on their front porches visiting with one another. Kids were running around the houses farther down Main Street, hoping their parents didn't realize the time.

Miss Daisy came out with her ever-present pad and took their orders. Everyone sat quietly, reflecting on the afternoon. Miss Daisy was back with some bread and a big pitcher.

"Here you go. You all look like you need this."

"Thanks Miss Daisy. I know I sure do. We found another dog at the farm, but this time he didn't make it," Dani told her.

"Oh, the poor dear! Marshall, you better catch this guy and soon. He deserves a horse whipping." Miss Daisy had the look now too.

He better call Nuggett and start combing the area or he'd have the residents out looking with pitchforks. He grabbed the pitcher of the Rose sisters' special iced tea and poured a glass for everyone.

"So, how is the investigation coming?" Mo asked next to him.

"I'm working with Sheriff Nuggett over in the next county. I'll need your help with some of this. We've created a map of both counties and where any calls have been made or any incidents have been reported. We're hoping to find a pattern and then guess where the fights could be. Some of the land is yours and some belongs to the Wyatts. I don't think we need to call in Will. Ashton Farm is farther away from the county line and so far the incidents are staying close to the line and haven't ventured far into either county," Marshall explained.

Everyone nodded and talked about the best time to look at the map. Katelyn kept glancing at Marshall out of the corner of her eye. They were all sitting close to each other and she could feel his leg brush up against hers every time one of them moved. To hide the blush staining her cheeks from the very vivid memory of their naked legs intertwined she took a large sip of the tea.

She looked around the table and saw that Dani was giving her a look. She raised her eyebrow and Dani shot a glance to Marshall and then smiled. Oh, God. Dani saw her checking out Marshall. She took another sip and refilled her glass. It gave her something to do that didn't involve looking at either of them. The tea tasted so good. One of these days she'd remember to ask Miss Daisy what she put in it.

"Here you all go." Miss Daisy brought out the dinner and placed it on the table.

"Okay. Enough of this sad talk. We don't get to hang out much, and I want to enjoy this beautiful night and try to get that horrible image out of my head. So, how about we change the subject? Marshall, are you dating anyone now?" Dani asked. She smiled when she saw the stunned looked on his face and Katelyn let loose with a nervous snicker.

"Um, no. You pregnant yet?" Katelyn got a close up view of a full smile that left her breathless.

"Touché." Dani saluted him with her glass of special tea and when she took a large sip everyone at the table had the answer to the pregnancy question.

"Your horses had a good showing at the Oaks and Derby this year, Mo."

Marshall shifted in his seat to look at Mo sitting next to him and Katelyn was thankful. The shift had brought his upper thigh to rest against hers and it felt so good. She took another drink and looked at his back. His strong, wide, muscular back.

"How are things going at the clinic?"

"What? Oh, good," she answered Dani and got a smirk back in return. "It's grown as Dr. Truett refuses to advance with technology. You know what they say about old dogs…"

"Very true. We took Brutus, my cat, to him once and while he didn't do anything wrong, I'd feel much more comfortable with you handling any surgery."

"Thank you, Dani. Hopefully, he'll never need it." Hm. She really needed to learn how to make this drink, because she was feeling really good right now and very, very happy.

"She's a great doctor. Bob gets to come see her next week for his check-up."

She almost sighed when he turned toward her. His thigh left hers, but the full length of his leg rested gently against hers. She could feel the curve of his calf and heat radiating from him. She leaned back and felt his arm. When he had turned he had apparently put his arm across the back of her chair. His hand cupped her shoulder and he started to draw little circles with his thumb on the back of her shoulder. The heat traveled straight to her... Oh.My.God.

She downed the rest of her drink and coughed. Marshall smiled at her and rubbed her back gently, which totally didn't help. Marshall turned away from her and back to Mo and Ahmed. She poured another glass of tea and took a sip to stop the coughing. She looked up and Dani was bright red, holding in her own laughter.

"I thought you were nice when I first met you."

"Sorry, I'll be good, I swear." Dani crossed her heart, but Katelyn didn't believe it for a second.

"How are Kenna and the baby?" Maybe if she changed subject Dani would behave.

"Doing great. Little Sienna is rolling over and just started eating baby cereal. Kenna and Will just dote on her constantly. I never suspected such a big man could be so gentle. It took him a little while to stop holding her like a football, but now he takes her everywhere and she happily rides along."

Katelyn turned toward the guys when she heard their laughter but got distracted by Marshall again. Her eyes were drawn down to the handcuffs nestled against his back. She took another drink of her tea and thought very dirty thoughts of what she wanted to do with those handcuffs.

"Katelyn? Are you okay? You're all flushed," Dani said loud enough for everyone to hear.

The whole table turned and stared at her. Could they tell what she was thinking? Was Father Francis going to pop up and tell her to hurry to confession, because God knew after the thought she just had, she'd be saying Hail Mary's for a month.

"Should I take you home?" Marshall asked.

She was pretty sure that smile wasn't one of comfort, but one of invitation.

"Yes!"

Marshall woke up and the room was still dark. Katelyn was nestled against him, her head using his arm as a pillow. He didn't know what he had done, but whatever it was it had worked. Katelyn was naked in bed with him again and it would be hard for her to sneak out of her own house.

He hadn't intended to spend the night with her. He was actually just hoping to ask her out on a date, but when he pulled up to her house she looked at him with such passion that he couldn't help himself. He had leaned over and kissed her, and then things escalated. They had gone up the back stairs to her room, kissing the whole way. It was a night he'd never forget.

His stomach growled and he tried to quiet it to no avail. Katelyn said that her grandparents were at the far end of the house, way away from her room and that they slept like rocks. Meaning, he should be pretty safe. He'd just head down the back stairs to the kitchen and grab a quick bite. He pulled his arm out from under Katelyn's head. He missed her contact almost immediately, but it also felt good to get some circulation back to his fingers.

He felt around for his pants but didn't feel them. He got up and, as his eyes adjusted, he looked around the room. Katelyn had a very feminine room. It was painted a pale yellow and had white furniture with pictures of flowers adorning the walls. On the far side of the room was an antique-looking desk and next to that he found his pants. Ruffles had them in her big fluffy pink bed. By the way her teeth were bared at him, she wasn't going to give them back without a fight.

He decided it would be better not to wake Katelyn so he slowly opened the door and stuck his head out into the dark hallway. Not a sound reached his ears. He slid out the door and down the back stairs. He turned at the bottom of the stairs and peeked into the kitchen. He grinned and breathed easy again, it was empty.

He snuck into the kitchen and as he passed the doorway he cursed as his toe connected with something hard. He looked down and crossed himself. He had run into the freaking cannonball! At least it didn't go off. He rounded the table and headed for the large stainless steel refrigerator.

He opened it up and blinked at the light. He grabbed a bottle of water and was taking a sip as he tried to decide what he wanted to eat when the main kitchen light came on.

"Oh my! That's not what I expected when I came to get a snack, but bless me, I won't complain."

"Mrs. Wyatt!" He practically jumped into the fridge and tried to hide behind the door.

"I was just going to make some warm milk."

Marshall turned, reached back, and grabbed the milk. Using it to shield himself he slid over to the island to hide safely behind it.

"Here you go ma'am."

"Why, thank you dear."

He waited until she turned to get a mug and then made a break for the stairs. This was the most embarrassing moment he'd ever had to endure. It made Army hazing look like amateur hour.

As he snuck back into bed with Katelyn, he hoped Mrs. Wyatt wouldn't say anything. Surely she wouldn't want to embarrass Katelyn. He slid his arm back under Katelyn's head and pulled her near. Having her next to him somehow calmed him. Most nights he was plagued with insomnia or nightmares from the war. But, with her near him, it was as if she kept them all at bay. He felt at peace. He closed his eyes and fell asleep instantly.

Chapter Eight

Katelyn's head pounded. Someone had to be operating a jackhammer in her room. Her eyes ached and it felt as though she was chewing on cotton. She was also very warm. She cracked her dry eyes and looked right into the sleeping face of the man she had spent the night dreaming about.

Apparently it was more than just a dream. She bit her pillow and groaned. Why did this keep happening? She looked down and groaned again, this time with frustration. The sheet was covering all the good parts. Well, there weren't really any bad parts.

"Good morning, Doc."

"Oh, you're awake." She looked around her room and was seriously considering going down the trellis outside her window.

"I'm surprised you're still here." He eyed the window too and she felt herself blush. "But, I'm glad you are. I was hoping you'd do me the honor of going out on a date with me."

Knock, knock.

"You've got to be kidding me! Quick, get under the bed." Katelyn shoved hard and caught a glimpse of the really good parts as she pushed him off the bed.

"I'm not going to hide under the bed like some teenager."

"Fine, then just lay there. No one can see you unless they come around the bed."

She saw him roll his eyes, but he stayed put. She grabbed her robe and went to answer the door.

"Good morning, dear!"

"Hi Nana, Papa. What are you all doing? Why do you have a vacuum? And why do you have a gun?"

"I'm on my way out to do some shooting. I just wanted to say good-bye to my precious, sweet, and only baby girl." Her grandfather showed her the twelve-gauge Parker Invincible shotgun and smiled.

"And I thought I'd just do some cleaning," her grandmother nearly sang as she plugged in the vacuum.

Her grandmother hadn't cleaned as long as Katelyn had known her. But that didn't stop her grandma from turning on the vacuum and attempting to vacuum the room. Katelyn bit her lip and looked nervously about as her grandfather smiled and her grandmother went straight to the far side of the bed. This was quickly turning into her worst nightmare.

"Beauford! I found a naked man. Well, you just don't find that every day. I thought there were just dust bunnies under beds. I guess I should clean more often."

Katelyn wanted to die. She saw Marshall stand up and grab a pillow to cover himself. The room was silent except for the sound of the shotgun being cocked.

"Well, Sweet Pea, it looks like you'll get your wish. You can help Katelyn plan a huge weddin'."

"Wedding?!" She shouted at the same time Marshall did.

"Now, Papa, this isn't what it looks like," Katelyn tried. She knew her grandparents were traditional, but they really weren't *that* traditional.

"Really, darlin'? Then just what is it?"

"Yeah, I'd like to know that too." Marshall grinned and she wondered again why she liked him.

"Well, it's… it's… well, dammit. It's just a one-night stand. For crying out loud, I'm a grown woman and can have a one-night stand without explaining it to everyone." She stomped her foot and suddenly felt seven again. "And, just because I have sex with someone doesn't mean I have to marry him! I'm pretty sure that practice was done away with during the feminist movement."

"Actually, Doc, it's been twice," Marshall put in.

"What?" She whirled around and glared at him. He was just standing there with a white pillow with roses on it over his best parts and a smile on his face. "Nana, stop staring!"

Her grandmother was standing slightly behind Marshall with a huge grin on her face as she got an eyeful of naked behind.

"We've slept together twice now. So, I don't think it can qualify as a one-night stand. You haven't forgotten our first time, have you?"

"Oh, I doubt a woman could forget that."

"Nana!" Katelyn stomped her foot again and then found herself rolling her eyes when Marshall gave her grandmother a wink. "You, stop encouraging her."

"Well, there you go. Twice. Come on Ruth, let's give the newlyweds some time to celebrate. They need to set a date after all." Her grandfather nodded his head and gestured to her grandmother to leave.

Her grandmother sighed wistfully as she took one last look at Marshall's behind. "You'll have a good marriage, if you know what I mean." With a wink she left Katelyn staring at a closed door. The sounds of her grandmother laughing out in the hall just rubbed salt into the wound.

"I think your grandparents played us." Marshall tossed the pillow back on the bed.

Katelyn blinked. Did this man have no shame? Apparently not as he wasn't in a hurry to cover up, not that she was complaining.

"I think they might have, too. I guess they saw your car out front. You should've left early in the morning. Now everyone is going to know about this!"

Katelyn rubbed the bridge of her nose. In just a couple of days she had given the town enough gossip to last a lifetime. Now, how was she going to get everyone to take her seriously?

"I guess I better get to work then. Since today is Saturday, I'm only working a half-day. How about I pick you up for dinner around seven? I know this great barbeque place in Lexington I thought we could hit up." Marshall grabbed his shirt off of the floor and slipped it on.

"No, I don't think so."

"What? Why not?" Marshall eyed his pants that Ruffles had curled up on.

"This was a mistake. It won't happen again. It was just a one-night stand."

He stopped his attempt to get Ruffles to move and gave her a look that could only be described as cocky.

"Fine, twice. Whatever, but it won't happen again. I'm having enough trouble being taken seriously in this town. The old guard sees me as some silly model and I'm constantly struggling against the rumors Truett and his gang are spreading. Now they'll just say I'm another conquest of the Davies brothers. Just another fallen bimbo." She felt her eyes start to tear up so she busied herself with pulling the white sheets and quilt up to finish making her bed.

"Katelyn, look, I know I was an ass to you when you first got to town. I was guilty of just the thing you were talking about. I thought you were just a blonde bimbo living off her father's money. I judged you based on who your father is and that was wrong of me. But, I've gotten to know you and you're not that cold person I thought you were."

"Gee, thanks. I think I'll stick with my decision not to do dinner." Katelyn hoped she sent him the coldest glare she had.

"That sounded bad, I'm sorry. I'm trying to say that by just spending a little time with you I've found that you're a smart, caring, passionate woman whom I'd like to get to know better. So, please, have dinner with me."

She thought about it for a second and even softened when she watched him trying to pull his pants out from under Ruffles. But she just couldn't be another notch on his belt.

"Thank you, but the answer is still no. You're just such a...," she waved her hand in front of her trying to think of right word, "man. You're such a man. I think you'd say anything to get into bed with a woman. So I don't hurt your delicate feelings, the sex was great, but I don't think we have anything else in common. Dinner would be a waste of time and all it would do is keep me front and center in the town gossip and hurt my business. Now, I need to get to the clinic. Come on Ruffles, let's go." Ruffles leapt up, surrendering the pants, and followed her as she made her escape.

Marshall pulled his pants on and glanced at the closed bedroom door. What just happened? They had shared another amazing night together and then she freaked out. Okay, so maybe he had a playboy reputation, but that shouldn't bother her. After all, he was more serious about her than any of those other girls.

And it wasn't like she had to worry about running into all his ex-girlfriends. He had done most of his dating in Lexington. He had to admit, he was at a loss. He had tried to do the right thing and ask her out properly to show her that this was more than a one, well, two-night stand.

He tucked his shirt in and strapped on his utility belt. Annie was going to give him so much shit for this when he got to work today. One thing Katelyn was right about—everyone would be talking about this. It was seven thirty and he was sure the whole town already knew his cruiser had sat outside the Wyatt house all night long. His fiery sister-in-law would be nothing compared to Paige though. Paige loved Katelyn and would descend on him almost as fast as John Wolfe, the notorious town gossip, could spread the word of where he spent the night.

He opened the door and looked down the hall. It was filled with portraits of old family members from Beauford and Ruth's families.

Needlepoints and other special heirlooms were framed in shadow boxes near the family member responsible for them. He thought about going down the back stairs again, but thought that would be the cowardly thing to do. And one thing he wasn't was a coward. Even though he was sure Beauford was at the bottom of the stairs with his shotgun, he was going to go out the front door and show Katelyn he wasn't afraid of the gossip and he was prepared to stick around. Now, if he only knew how to get her to agree to a date.

Marshall went down the stairs and was heading for the front door when he was stopped.

"Son, come in here a minute." Beauford called to him from his office.

Marshall walked into the room. Ruffles raised her head from the couch and growled, which prompted Alice, who was curled up next to her, to do the same.

"Oh hush girls. Go see Mommy, the men need to talk."

Alice instantly leapt up and, with her beautiful pink collar around her scarred neck, wagged her tail and headed for the kitchen. Ruffles gave one last glare and then followed behind. Beauford closed the heavy wooden door and headed to his desk.

"Now, son, just what in the devil do you think you're doing?"

"Sir?"

"Are you trying to get yourself shot? You do realize I'll shoot you if you hurt my granddaughter. The only reason I haven't already is because I think the rogue is about to be tamed. I could tell by the goofy look on your face this morning that you like my granddaughter. So, tell me what you think you're doing jumping into bed with her before courting her properly?" Beauford asked, leaning back in his old leather chair.

"I'm trying to do things properly, so to say. I asked her out on a date and she refused."

"Oh dear. It appears she's more like her grandmother than I thought. I met Ruthie in a political lecture my senior year at Emory. She was so beautiful and so smart. I tried to talk to her after class. I offered to tutor her and she informed me that she was available to tutor me, seeing as she had the highest grade in the class. Then she spun around and took off in a cherry red 1950 Cadillac convertible. I chased after her the entire school year. She kept turning me down. All it did was make me work harder in school to impress her and you know what?"

"What?"

"I married her, didn't I?" Beauford smiled wide.

"So, you suggest I just don't give up?" Marshall didn't know how much help that advice really was.

"That, and you need to change your approach. Katelyn likes to think she's a modern woman, but she's traditional at heart. Ruthie just wanted to be wooed and the second I did it right, she married me faster than a gnat can blink. I guarantee you, you give Katelyn some romantic gentlemanly attention and she'll come around."

Marshall tried to hide his reaction. He knew Beauford and Ruth were in the wrong generation, but who was he to need advice? He didn't want to brag, but didn't Beauford know of his reputation? But then again, nothing had worked so far.

"Well, thank you, sir. I'll work on it." Marshall turned and started to open the closed office door.

"Oh, and son..." Beauford stood up from his chair and placed his shotgun on his desk. "If I find you naked in my house again, I will shoot you."

Chapter Nine

Marshall dodged the stapler flying through the air at him. It crashed against the empty jail cell and fell harmlessly to the ground.

"Annie!"

"Don't you Annie me. You're in deep trouble." He watched his sister-in-law grab the tape dispenser and throw it with painful accuracy. "So, what are you going to do about it? And the answer better be good, because I'll go for my taser next."

"I asked her out and she turned me down."

"Oh come on! You aren't going to take no for an answer now are you?" She pulled out her taser and turned it on.

"No! No I am not. I'm trying to *woo* her as Beauford calls it. I just don't exactly know how. It's not like I do this every day." He held up his hands and took a step back.

He couldn't do anything, like tackle or disarm Annie or Cade would kill him. Not counting what Paige would do too, and quite frankly, Paige was scarier than all his brothers when worked up. It also wasn't a good sign when Annie narrowed her eyes like she just did. His deputy had a little bit of a temper, which happened to only get worse with pregnancy. The consequential good news being that the Belles might be slowing their visits to the office.

"Oh, that's right! You never had a woman with enough brains to turn you down. You always slummed it with the ones that fell at your feet. Now you have a real woman and you don't know what to do. It's just plain pathetic! You make me sick Davies."

"Jesus Annie. That's harsh."

"No, I mean, you really make me sick. Damn morning sickness. Don't think I'm done with you yet, Davies. I'm not letting you off the hook so easily," she called as she ran for the bathroom.

Well, it was now or never to make his escape. It was time for breakfast and after last night with Katelyn, he needed it. He allowed himself a little macho grin before heading upstairs from the jail. Marshall pushed open the glass side doors of the courthouse and stopped at one of the two stoplights in town as he waited for a car to pass before heading across the street.

June was always beautiful. Flowers lined Main Street. Shop doors were open and colorful decorations adorned the shop windows. It was hot, and getting hotter as July approached, but everyone was outside enjoying the days before July and her humidity came to town. New American flags had just been hung in preparation for the big July Fourth weekend celebration.

Every year Keeneston held a small Independence Day Celebration. The streets were closed and there was a huge cookout on Main Street. There were games for the kids and the annual BBQ cook-off and pie contest. It was just a couple of weeks away and he was already excited for it.

Marshall walked through the open door of the café and went straight to the table in the back. Maybe no one would see him back there.

"I hear you're having lady troubles." The old southern drawl of Roger Burns cut through the chatter and silenced the place.

He should've known better — he *did* know better than to come here and expect to be left alone.

"Nothing I can't handle." He shot a confident grin to the old man and tried to make it to his table.

"That's not what we heard." Miss Daisy stood with her hands on her thin hips in the middle of a sea of bobbing heads.

"That's right. We heard she turned you down and is refusing to go out on date with you," Miss Violet said as she poked her cheery, round face out from the kitchen.

"We heard you had no game," Paul Russell laughed from his seat next to his great-uncle Roger. "I think it's time for another Davies brother to lose to me. I might just go out and pay a call to Katelyn today."

"If I recall, Paul, you may have beaten us at baseball, but you struck out when it came to women," Marshall snapped.

Paul had been a rival of his all through high school. They had competed for starting lineups and women. For his part, Marshall cared more about the women and was undefeated in that arena. And he intended things to stay that way. Paul didn't get Kenna from Will and now she was an Ashton. He intended to take a play out of his friend's playbook — that is if he could ever get her to go out on a date with them.

"I think you're perfect just the way you are. And I bet your…game… is outstanding." Nancy slithered her way over to him and managed to laugh, pout, and press her breast against his arm all at the same time.

"Thanks for your, um, support Nancy." He pulled away and took a seat in his booth.

"What you need is a plan. Real, good, smart women need more than the… game… you're offering." Miss Daisy whipped out her pad and started to take notes. "Flowers. Every man must start with flowers."

"That's right, and not just any flowers."

Edith's comments were met with a bunch of positive nods of heads and 'that's rights'. Edith had been married for almost sixty years before her husband passed away, so he guessed she'd know.

"Yes indeedy. What type of flower you give sets the whole stage." Miss Lily popped out of the back with a tray of food to take to the bed and breakfast.

"It does?"

"That's right. Each flower has a meaning. My name for example, I was named after the calla lily, which means regal. Daisy means innocence, and Violet means faithfulness. Pink roses mean friendship, so you probably want to stay away from that."

"Come on, women don't read into the type of flowers you give them."

All the women in the café chorused, "Yes we do."

"We got a 9-1-1 for you out at the peewee soccer match." Annie's voice crackled over the radio. "And don't think you're off the hook."

He knew better than to think that. He grabbed a bagel off Miss Lily's plate, gave her a quick peck on the cheek and a wink before heading to the soccer fields. The last 9-1-1 call from there was about a couple parents from both teams starting a shoving match.

Marshall pulled up to the fields and walked over to the bleachers. The referee was still alive. There were no bodies being flung against the sides of minivans. He scanned the crowd; no one seemed to be fighting.

"Sheriff! Yoo-hoo! Over here." Pam Gilbert stood and waved from the middle of the bleachers.

"Morning, Pam. What's the problem here?"

"It's not our problem, it's your problem. We've all been talking about your dating issues and we have a suggestion." Pam indicated that all of the parents from Keeneston, and probably a few from the Nicholasville team had also contributed in the dissection of his relationship with Katelyn.

"This isn't an emergency Pam and 9-1-1 is an emergency number only," he chided to absolutely no avail. Pam seemed utterly unfazed.

"Now sit down here and let's talk it out." She patted the seat next to her and then stood to cheer as one of her kids kicked the ball.

"I don't have time for this."

"Sit!" Pam snapped her fingers and gave him the look that said he'd get a time out if he didn't sit down right now.

"Okay, make it quick." He sat down on the bleacher and waited for the torture to start.

"You need to be domestic."

"What the hell does that mean?"

"Cook for her, in a *clean* house. Preferably one that you actually cleaned yourself."

"What does this have to do with anything?" He snapped. By the look Pam sent him he better check his attitude or he might end up grounded.

"Women want to see that a man is ready for a commitment and a mature relationship. A man who has a messy house, doesn't cook, doesn't do laundry, and gallivants around town clearly isn't ready for a serious relationship."

"Oh. That actually makes sense, more so than the flowers and all their meanings."

"You better pay attention. My husband brought me striped carnations when we first met." The women in the bleachers gasped. "I know, right? It means refusal. I thought he was breaking up with me."

Marshall looked over at Pam's husband who just nodded and shrugged his shoulders and said, "I learned. So will you," before turning back to the game.

"We've got another 9-1-1." Annie interrupted.

"What is it?" He asked into his radio.

"It's at Kenna's law office."

"Okay. I'll be right there."

"Thanks for the advice. It was actually insightful."

He waved good-bye and leaped into his cruiser. Too much had gone down in Kenna's law office in the past for this to be good. Between Henry's defense clients and Kenna also being a prosecutor, things could get heated on occasion. But today was Saturday. No one should be at the office. Hopefully it wasn't a fire.

Marshall slid to a stop and jumped out of the cruiser. There didn't appear to be any smoke coming out of it. There weren't any broken windows or any other damage that he could see. He walked to the glass door and easily pulled it open. The office wasn't locked?

"Hello?"

"Marshall? We're back here." Henry's voice came from his office in the back.

Marshall passed through the lobby and turned left towards the offices. Henry's office was first and then Kenna's was closer to the library in the back.

"I got an emergency call. What's going on?"

He walked into Henry's office and found him behind his desk and Kenna seated on the couch. Stacks of papers and books surrounded them both.

"Hi Marshall."

"Kenna." He leaned down and placed a kiss on her cheek. "How's Sienna doing?"

"She's growing too fast," she beamed. "Thanks for asking."

"Now, can you please tell me what the emergency was?" Marshall put his hands on his hips and tried for his most intimidating glare.

"You are." Henry put down his pen and leaned back in his brown leather chair. "We hear you're having some major dating problems. The word on the street is that you got shot down and you have no idea how to get back in the saddle."

"Jeez Henry, could you fit in any more clichés into that sentence?"

"Laugh it up. While you're sitting at number two on the Top Bachelor's List of Keeneston and getting shot down, I, way down at number five, have a date with a Keeneston Belle. So, take my advice and walk up to Katelyn and say the following."

Henry stood up, did an eyebrow wiggle, put his hands in his pockets and walked over to him. Marshall couldn't decide which to do, laugh or hide behind Kenna.

"You walk up to her, confidently, like this. Then you look into her eyes, like this, and say, 'Baby, I'll make you dinner if you make me breakfast." He wiggled his eyebrows again and Marshall couldn't help the laughing.

"Are you serious?"

"It works. You gotta get some game or you won't be number two for long. I'm charging up the polls!"

"The best advice I have is to not listen to Henry. Just be yourself and ask her out. It may also help to burn all your little black books and make it clear to everyone in town you're no longer available. Katelyn is a sweet woman. She won't say yes if she thinks you're either playing the field or if she's getting in the way of an already budding relationship."

"Sheriff, we got a 9-1-1 call from your sister's shop." Dinky's voice came through his radio.

"Is it already past noon?"

"Yes, Sir. Deputy Davies went home about thirty minutes ago. What would you like me to do about the 9-1-1?"

"Send Noodle on all remaining 9-1-1 calls. I'm taking the rest of the day off and will be unreachable except in a serious emergency as deemed by blood and bodily injury. Got it?"

"Yes, Sir. If I may, real quick, women like it when you speak from the heart."

Marshall turned down the volume to his radio and headed out the door. This was just getting to be too much.

Katelyn patted the Australian Shepherd on his head and handed the leash back to his owner. Tex had sliced his foot when he was out helping round up some cattle on the Pitterman's farm. Mrs. Pitterman was a woman in her early sixties. Her mousy brown hair was streaked with gray and her face tanned from hours spent outside tending to the farm.

"Thank you for seeing us so quickly. Honestly, I didn't know what to expect, with what they are saying about you around town," Mrs. Pitterman said as she gathered her things.

"Saying, about me?" Was Dr. Truett saying bad stuff about her again?

"Well, there's that rumor that you bought your degree and don't know what you're doing, but enough people have seen you and assured me you were very competent. No, no, I was worried about the fact that you're spending the night with all these different men. I'm a good church-going woman and some are saying you're not a good role model for Keeneston top bachelorette. There's some talk of a revote. But, you're not bad at all. You were very kind to Tex and so thoughtful to get us in immediately because you know we use him for our work. Thank you for that. I'll stand against the revote. But, if you don't mind me saying, you may want to keep the barn door closed for a while, if you get my meaning."

Katelyn stood still and was speechless for a moment. "Different men?"

"Well, yes. Men. Everyone knows about that man you took home after Cade and Annie's wedding and then Marshall just the other night. Who knows who else there's been. My church's sewing circle is all abuzz about it."

"Really? About me?"

"Yes, it died down for a while, but the rumor mill is flying again with you being named on the top of the bachelorette list. But, like I said, I'll try to tame them as much as possible. Thank you again for fixin' Tex up right quick."

"You're welcome. Have a good day and let me know if Tex needs anything else." Katelyn pasted on her best commercial photo-shoot smile and walked her client out front to Shelly's desk before saying her final good bye. She managed to pretend everything was fine until she got to her office in the back. Tears gathered as she hung her head and typed in her notes on Tex. Great, not only is she a phony, she's now the town slut.

She was using her fingers to wipe away her tears when she heard the door swing open. She didn't want to see anyone right now and she just wanted to bury herself in paperwork and escape home in the dead of the night so she didn't have to encounter anyone.

"So, you've finally heard." Shelly put her arm around her shoulders and Katelyn felt the dam broke.

"I can't believe people are saying these things about me."

"I, and others, have done our best to stop the rumors. It seems as soon as we stomp one out, another one pops up. Someone is determined to pin a scarlet letter on you."

"Great. Just what I need as I'm trying to establish myself here and be taken seriously." Katelyn stopped when she heard the late night bell ring.

"I'll get it. Then I need to head home. Call me if you need anything. The kids are in bed by nine, and then I'm all yours."

"Thanks, Shelly."

Katelyn locked up the back office with all the medicines and headed for the front office. Bekah was in the back feeding the overnight boarders and had already locked up. Katelyn went to set the alarm, but noticed a large beautiful white orchid sitting on top of Shelly's desk. A white envelope was leaning against it, her name sprawled across the front of it masculine writing.

Doc —

I saw these and thought of you. Please know I am thinking of you and hope you will agree to have dinner with me when you are ready.

— Marshall

She read the card twice. Was this really Marshall? He couldn't possibly feel like this. He was always so cocky and was such a playboy. He probably had someone else write it. It was late and she was too tired to think about it. At least she had flowers now, and she guessed the thought was what counted.

Chapter Ten

The night air was static with energy. The anticipation thick and heavy as it rose with every fight. Thunder clapped and deafened the night air as a summer storm raged outside. But no one heard it. They were all in an old barn far out in the country and were too busy watching the fights in the ring. The place was packed. She couldn't have been happier. She turned to her partner and smiled.

"You did a great job Camille. Turnout is wonderful," she yelled to the fight organizer.

"Thanks. Without ya'll's info, we'd never know about this place. How are the bets going?"

"Real well. We've made around thirty grand so far and the big fight is yet to come. I think we'll make out with around fifty grand after we take our cut of the gun money and after the payout to the winner."

"Great. I need to go get Romeo ready for his fight. I hope that representative from International is here. Tonight has been perfect."

The crowd erupted as first blood was drawn in the ring. She nodded in response to Camille. This would be their crowning glory if they could pull it off. All four of them would go onto the next level. Good-bye rural South, hello Europe.

She didn't have dogs. She was the money girl. She could run numbers faster than anyone around. She was one of the most sought after bookies and had worked hard to earn the reputation as being one of the most elite and respected ones in the South. No one messed with her, she had all the names of the fighters, the dealers, and the gamblers—and they all knew she'd use them in a second if they screwed her. They also knew she protected those names with her life and that's why they trusted her.

She looked back at the ring as the shouts matched the thunder pounding the skies. As soon as the first blood was drawn, the crowd became just as bloodthirsty as the beasts in the ring. The metallic smell of blood filled the arena and drove the frenzy further toward madness.

The dogs picked up on the madness and the violence escalated rapidly. The bigger dog went in for the kill. His powerful jaws locked around the smaller dog's neck and clamped down tight. The windpipe of the smaller dog was crushed and with a quick adjustment the bigger dog moved his jaws to the scruff of the neck where in one powerful move he shook his head and tried to snap the neck.

The smaller dog was sent flying across the ring and the crowd was barely contained. They pushed and shoved to get a better view of the kill. Their bodies pressed against the side of the wooden ring as they cheered. The small dog lay fatally wounded and waited for the end as his death was applauded.

★　　★　　★

Marshall looked at the normally cheerful building and knew the colorful petunias were really just camouflage for the scariest and most efficient interrogators he'd ever come across. He took a deep breath, squared his shoulders, and went to face the music.

"Hey Sheriff," Miss Daisy said sweetly as she poured him a cup of coffee. "How are you doing this morning?"

"I'm doing well, you?" he asked as he took a sip of his coffee and waited for the questions to begin.

"We heard you dropped off an orchid last night at the vet clinic," Miss Daisy said.

It was phrased as a statement, but it was really a question. He decided not to respond and just took another sip of his coffee. He knew better than to think that would be the end of it, but he thought he'd make them work for it a little.

"That's right, Daisy Mae. I heard they were beautiful. I also heard there was a note." Miss Violet poked her flour-covered nose out from the kitchen.

"Um-hm, I heard it wasn't just any note, but a handwritten note," Daisy added in.

"Did you hear that it took him a full fifteen minutes to write it when he was at the flower shop?"

"I didn't hear that, Violet Fae. I wonder what took him so long to write it."

Marshall hid his smile behind his cup and wondered how long they'd go on. As more people came in, more rumors floated around him. Nancy glided in looking fresh and all too perky in some kind of dressy thing.

"Good morning, Sheriff. So sorry about last night." She took a seat next to him and waved Miss Daisy over for a cup of coffee.

"Excuse me?"

"I heard that Katelyn didn't even care about that beautiful orchid you sent. I heard she said it was pathetic compared to the huge bouquets she's used to receiving from her admirers."

The audible gasp from the patrons told him that Nancy was the first one to have this bit of gossip. He wanted to dismiss it as out of hand, but it still nagged at him. Katelyn was beautiful. She was a supermodel and he'd been insane to think she'd want to settle for a local sheriff. Maybe Nancy was right.

The door chimed and he instinctually looked to see who was walking in. Dressed in a similar brown uniform, Sheriff Nuggett came through the door and scanned the crowd until spotting him.

"Nuggett." He nodded. "Excuse us Nancy, would ya?"

"Of course! I understand — men's business. I hope I get to see you at the Belle Ball. You should be receiving your invitation soon. Have a good meeting gentlemen." Nancy got up from the table gave a little finger wave before taking a seat at a nearby table with Jasmine.

"What's up?" Marshall asked as soon as they were alone.

"We've had reports of two missing dogs."

"Like missing people?"

"Yes. Our local vet got a call from two of his clients frantic about their missing dogs. They were hoping they had been dropped off at the vet clinic. The humane society hadn't picked up any dogs of that description."

"Could they have just run away?"

"Unlikely. Both were house pets with no history of running away and the key fact was that both dogs were in yards with electric fences. Their collars had been removed and were left in the yard."

"Damn." Marshall rubbed his hand over his head. He couldn't imagine the fear those dogs and owners must be going through.

"Exactly. They're escalating. I've looked at the map you sent over and found a couple of areas worth looking into."

"I have too. I also have a long list of suspects. I'll email my notes over to you." Marshall pulled out his phone and sent the notes to Nuggett right then. "You think we missed the fight already?"

"Unfortunately. But I'm going to do some driving around tonight and see what I can find."

"How about I ride along with you. There's some places here I'd like to check out right on the county line. It may be easier if we work on this together so there are no jurisdictional issues."

"Sounds good. I'll pick you up at nine tonight. And, if you don't mind, can I give you some advice?"

"Of course. I've been a sheriff for a couple months, you've been one for a decade. I'm always learning."

"My advice is about you and this gal. I heard you gave her flowers. Good move. The note was a good touch too. But, I'd make sure you get some face-to-face time this evening so you stay fresh in her mind and show her you're determined. I had to work for my wife, but it was worth it." Nuggett stood and put on his hat. "I'll see you tonight."

"See you then, and thanks for the advice."

Geez. His dating life was now gossip in multiple counties. What was next, the front page of the newspaper? Local television news coverage?

"Hi Sheriff," Jasmine's voice purred from behind him.

Oh great, both Nancy and Jasmine in the same day. Was it too much to hope she would've stayed at her own table? Were all the Belles going to pounce on him today? Whereas Nancy liked to show what a perfect political wife she'd be, Jasmine liked to show what an, um, attentive wife she'd be.

Jasmine fluffed her dyed red hair and pushed her very ample breasts forward after taking the seat Nuggett just vacated. Before he could tell her he was about to leave, her hand was on his thigh, gently moving up and down over his uniform.

"Oooh, Sheriff, I'm so sorry about things not working out with that girl. But, she's a horrid, snooty, amazon of a woman. And so cold. Not warm, pliable, or responsive at all. I think you're lucky it didn't work out," she leaned in and whispered seductively into his ear, her warm breath dancing over his lobe.

"Jas," he stood up quickly from his chair and dropped a five on the table, "I appreciate your concern, but Katelyn is neither horrid nor cold or any of those other things you have said and I'd appreciate it if you kept your unwanted opinions to yourself."

He knew he had taken her to task, but he was tired of hearing the Belles trash Katelyn. He'd apologize for snapping at her eventually, but not today. He nodded to Miss Daisy and Miss Violet as they stood staring open-mouthed at his rude behavior. By tonight, his mother would be over having something to say about his manners.

Katelyn had never had so many clients in one day. Every pet owner in Keeneston found an excuse to stop by and they all stood huddled around the orchid next to Sally's desk. She had taken the note home with her. Some silly part of her had tucked it away in her keepsake box.

Each client asked about the note she had received as she examined their pet. Every person was trying to get the scoop, trying to find out what was in the note. It would've been humorous if it wasn't so invasive. However, in this one day she'd be able to make the monthly payment on all her new equipment!

"Did you hear Sheriff Nuggett had a meeting with Marshall this morning?" Shelly asked as Katelyn handed the last bit of paperwork to her.

"No. I didn't. All the talk I heard today was about the orchid and the note. More people wanting to know what was written in the note."

"So, what was in the note?" Shelly pried.

"I don't know why it matters, it's not like he actually wrote it."

"You don't know that. The word around town is he wrote it himself at the flower shop."

Katelyn ignored her friend's stare and thought about what she had said. She wondered if something else had happened. Why else would Sheriff Nuggett come meet with him?

"What did Sheriff Nuggett say? Did something happen?" Katelyn prayed that another dog wasn't found.

"I don't know. They're staying pretty tight-lipped about it." Shelly looked at the clock on the wall and grimaced. "I better get going. Today flew by and I need to pick up a pizza on the way home. It's past seven so the husband and kids are probably fighting each other for the leftovers like wild animals by now. I'll see you tomorrow."

"Bye Shelly. Thanks for staying late. I really appreciate it." Katelyn waited for her best friend to leave and then grabbed her purse. She wanted to find out what that meeting was about.

Marshall and Bob were on the couch having some bonding time. Bob's copper-colored coat stuck out against the dark walnut furniture. His head was leaning against Marshall's shoulder as they watched Animal Planet. Bob growled and barked when the Turtleman dove under water and brought up a snapping turtle with his bare hands.

"We need to call him and have him get the snapping turtles in our pond, don't we?" Marshall asked his best friend.

Bob wagged his tail. He'd be up for anything that meant those turtles were gone. They had been tormenting him for months. The other week Bob was chasing some ducks down by the pond and Marshall had seen him run into the water just to turn around and run as fast as he could out of there with a big turtle chasing after him.

He rubbed Bob's belly and turned back to the show he'd only been half watching. The rest of the time, he was either thinking about the case or Katelyn. He was stuck with what to do next with her, but he was pretty sure he had a good place to start in the investigation. In sharing the information with Nuggett, it was interesting to see where the fights took place, but more interestingly where they did not take place.

He wanted to talk to Nuggett about it tonight. It seemed these people were cruel, but not stupid. They wouldn't have the fights on their property, so if they eliminated the areas where the known fights and dog thefts were, it would actually show them the area the criminals lived in. Then he'd pull the arrest records for that area and hopefully be able to narrow it down to a couple suspects.

Bob cocked his head at the sound of the doorbell, but decided Animal Planet was more interesting. Marshall glanced at the clock. Nuggett was over an hour early. He pushed himself off the couch to Bob's grunts and groans of dissatisfaction at his human pillow leaving.

"You're early," he said as he opened the door.

"I didn't know you were expecting me."

"Katelyn." He blinked and looked again making sure he wasn't dreaming. "I'm sorry, I thought you were Sheriff Nuggett. Please, come in."

Marshall opened the door wide and allowed her into his old farmhouse. Miles had gone for style while he had gone for comfort. His house was old and the antique furniture reflected that. His house had been the bachelor pad for the longest time, but one by one they had all moved out. Miles' house had been built and furnished, Cade had gotten married and renovated his house, and Cy was just never there.

Bob raised his head from the couch and stared at Katelyn for a minute before putting his head back down and turning back to the show. Katelyn smiled and shook her head.

"I guess I'm not worth the effort," Katelyn joked.

"I think you are," Marshall said softly.

"Thank you."

He liked the way Katelyn blushed at his compliment. Maybe the flowers had worked! He led her into the open living room and sat down with her on a loveseat.

"I hope you don't think I'm prying, but I wanted to ask you about the café this morning."

"Nothing happened with Nancy or Jasmine. I'm not interested in any other women and have made sure they know that. Actually, I'm pretty sure Jasmine may not talk to me again. I was pretty rude when I made it known that I was interested in you, not her."

Katelyn's mouth turned into a pretty O shape as she batted her blue eyes a couple of time. He could see a range of emotions flash across her eyes.

"That's nice. I don't really know what to say to that."

"I just wanted you to know I'm serious about wanting a date with you. I won't be doing any of my playboy games where I date multiple women at once. You're all I want."

"This is embarrassing, but I was talking about your meeting with Sheriff Nuggett. Although," she added quickly, "it is very good to know that I won't be lost in your harem."

"Um, well, umm. I guess I really stepped in it, huh?" Marshall laughed.

He didn't know what else to do. He better just throw in the towel. There would be no way she'd agree to a date now.

"I guess that's a no to dinner then?" He shook his head. Wow, he had blown it.

"I didn't say that."

Her quiet voice reached his ears and he perked up. Was she saying yes?

"So you will go out on a date with me?"

"I didn't say that either." She smiled and he felt his insides go to mush at the same time he wanted to jump in the air and pump his fists. He wasn't out of the game yet!

"The reason I came was to find out what's going on with the dog-fighting ring. I was so worried Sheriff Nuggett had found another dog."

"Not exactly. Two dogs were reported missing. Stolen, actually. Their electric collars had been taken off and left in the yard. We're going out tonight to look into some of the areas that are suspicious to us."

"That's the trouble with below ground electrical fences. They keep your dog in, but they don't keep anything out. I hope they're found, but I'm afraid they won't be. Good luck tonight and, please, do be careful."

"Come on Doc, don't tell me you're starting to care about what happens to me," he winked. He was rewarded with a smile, but she didn't say anything more. "Katelyn, I..."

Marshall was interrupted by the knock on the door. He apologized for the interruption and went to open the door. His mother stood in all her glory at the door. Her hands were full of homemade goodies and she probably carried a couple of women's numbers who wanted to settle down and get married in her pocket.

"Ma. What are you doing here?"

Marcy Davies pushed her way past him and headed into the house. There was no stopping his mother once she got a whiff of possible bride potential. Marcy made a beeline right for Katelyn who stood as soon as she saw his mother.

"Katelyn, dear, I didn't know you were here. I'm so sorry to interrupt. But, since I have you here, there's something I wanted to ask you."

"Yes, ma'am?" Katelyn smiled. Marcy Davies was the mother she always wished she had. She was attentive, loving, caring, and never disappeared for months at a time.

"I wanted to invite you and your grandparents over to dinner next Sunday night. Please tell me ya'll can make it."

"I will check with my grandparents and let you know. Thank you so much for the offer. I know I'm free."

"Wonderful! I'll just put this in the kitchen. I don't want to be in the way." Marcy gave her a wink and headed to the kitchen as Marshall started grabbing food from her overladen arms.

Marshall walked his mother to the door and gave her a kiss on her cheek. Katelyn had promised to call her in the morning to let her know if her grandparents would be joining them for their weekly family dinner. He opened the door and walked out onto the porch and down the white wooden steps.

"I wanted to apologize again for interrupting."

"No you don't, Ma. I'm pretty sure it was part of a well thought out plan."

"Well, I did hear you were having trouble getting a date, and well, now you have one!" His mother cupped his faced gently, "We mothers are good for some things you know."

"You're good for many things. Good night Ma."

Marshall waved good-bye to his mother and when he turned around Katelyn was standing at the door. She had a wistful look on her face, but her purse hung from her hand.

"You heading out too?"

"Yes. I'm sure Sheriff Nuggett will be here soon and it sounds like you have a long night ahead of you."

Marshall looked up at her from the bottom of the stairs. Her long sun-kissed hair was draped over her shoulders and down to her breasts. She was so beautiful. He needed to make sure he thanked his mother for finally helping him get a kinda sorta date. He looked at his watch and hurried into the house. He needed to get his gear ready before Nuggett got here in ten minutes. He had a couple suspects he wanted to check out.

Chapter Eleven

Katelyn batted her eyelashes and puckered her lips. She was in heaven. It had been a long day at work. She was still jam-packed with new clients wanting gossip more than needing medical care for their pets. At least she was able to get most of the dogs and cats in town up to date on shots or set up to be spayed or neutered.

The workload wasn't the exhausting part. The exhausting part was trying to field all the questions about her dating life. It had progressed from hearing about Marshall to being asked out by most of her single male clients. Apparently people were taking notice of that stupid Keeneston Bachelor/Bachelorette list. And the floodgates opened when they found out she wasn't officially dating anyone.

She had quickly exited though the back door and headed over to Paige's shop for some retail therapy. She looked back into the mirror at the large-brimmed pastel pink hat that sloped gently down and covered one eye. It was so Marilyn Monroe.

"That looks great on you!" Paige said as she came out of the back room holding another hat in her hand.

"Thanks, but it's all the hat. I guess I inherited my grandmother's love of hats. They're just so much fun!"

"I heard you had a lot of fun today. How many numbers did you get?" Paige ribbed her.

"It was horrible. You know I'm not one of those open people. I don't talk about my feelings and I don't do public displays of affection, and I certainly won't talk about what I'm feeling, who I want to date, or play flirty doctor with my clients."

Katelyn felt much better with that quick venting. Shelly and Paige understood her and never made her feel judged. She could really talk to them.

"I heard that all the bachelors are getting attention from this list. And I'm pretty sure the other bachelorettes are trying to nab their top counterparts. At least I know Nancy and Jasmine have both been hanging around my brothers. Kenna told me they even stopped by the law office and now have dates with Henry. Dani said they've even made their way out to the farm looking for Ahmed, only to turn tail and race back to Keeneston when he leveled a look at them."

"I had no idea anyone actually took this list seriously." Katelyn shook her head. Who cared about being on a stupid list?

"It's a huge deal. But, what about you and Marshall? Maybe you won't be eligible for the list next year?" Paige nudged her and laughed at the surprised look on her face.

"No. There's nothing between us."

"Right, and there were no flowers."

"It's no big deal. We're just working on this investigation. There are no romantic feelings there."

Liar liar pants on fire went through Katelyn's mind as soon as she said it. She didn't know what she was feeling, but it certainly wasn't professionalism. And those stupid flashbacks to Marshall lying naked in her bed were nothing either.

"Oh, I'm so relieved then," Paige said on an exhale.

"What? Why?" Katelyn couldn't contain the surprise in her voice. Was she not good enough for Marshall?

"Well, I heard that Kandi was on him like a tick on a deer. If you were to get in between her and her prey, she'd be liable to do something mean and I'd hate to see you get hurt. Kandi is so petty and vicious. She wouldn't stop at anything to get you out of the picture. I had thought, incorrectly I guess, that Marshall was down the café waiting for you, but I guess he's waiting for someone else. I sure hope he has more sense than to be waiting for Kandi!" Paige handed her a yellow hat with long white netting for her to try on.

Images of Kandi fawning over Marshall flooded her head. Her hand closed to a fist as she felt her heartbeat speed up. She was flush and her breath was coming faster. What was the matter with her?

Anger, nothing but pure anger and jealousy had come over her at the thought of Marshall in Kandi's arms and more importantly waking up in her bed. Kandi already had one husband, she sure as hell wasn't going to take the one man that mattered enough to Katelyn to feel jealous.

"I'm sorry, I think I need to get going and pick up dinner. It's been a long day,"

Katelyn had never felt such feelings in her life. She must be having a panic attack because her anxiety was getting worse as her mind refused to slow down. Images of Kandi running her hands over his body, images of Kandi's balloons bouncing as she rode...oh God, she had to hurry before Kandi got those long manicured nails sunk into Marshall.

"Are you okay? You look sick." Paige told her.

"No, no. I'm fine, just hungry. See you later."

Katelyn ripped off the hat and tossed it back to Paige. She grabbed her purse and was out the door before Paige could say another word. She ate up the sidewalk with her long strides, her eyes never leaving the flower baskets sitting outside the door of the café. She only made it half way to the café before she crossed the street. People were trying to talk to her so she just waved to them as she passed, that is, if and when she even heard them.

The café was getting closer and her vision was tunneled. She didn't hear the birds, or the people on the street. All her thoughts were of what was waiting for her beyond the doors. Was Marshall a willing participant or just another man caught in Kandi's web?

Finally! She pushed open the glass door and charged into the ̃fé. She stopped and looked around to locate him. Her breathing ̃elaxed and the elephant that had been sitting on her chest stood up. Marshall was there alright, but he was alone. He was sitting at the back booth with his back to the door and his laptop in front of him. He was working. Alone.

Okay, it was finally time to admit that maybe she felt something for him more than just lust. There's no way she'd act like this if she didn't have some kind of attachment to him. So, maybe it was time to find out exactly what those feelings were. Katelyn started forward to where Marshall was bent over his computer.

"How does one manage to be both an ice princess and a slut? Now get out of my way."

Katelyn felt hands on her shoulder and then a push all before she knew what was going on. She tripped forward and into the back of Judge Cooper, the district and family court judge in Keeneston. She looked up at Kandi's smirking face as she shot her a triumphant look from the head of Marshall's table.

"I'm so sorry, Judge."

"It's alright, sweetheart. Are you okay?" The older, stoic man asked.

Katelyn looked over and watched Kandi in her skin-tight white tank top and mini blue jean skirt fawning over Marshall. Kandi leaned over the table and closed his laptop, giving him an eyeful of her candies. Katelyn watched as she reached across the table and ran her hand down his arm, sticking her overblown cleavage even closer to his face. Kandi looked up at her and winked. Rage burst forward and for once she decided there was no need to temper it.

"I will be, in just a minute, thank you. May I borrow that piece of blueberry pie, your honor?"

"Sure, hon." Judge Cooper handed her the large piece of deep purple pie.

"Thank you so much." She smiled at him and, with a calm she'd never felt before, walked straight to Marshall's table.

"Excuse me," she drawled in her most polite southern accent with all the charm of the Deep South her grandmother had taught her.

Kandi turned on her with fire in her narrowed eyes. Her overly mascaraed eyelashes twitched like a hundred spider legs. She waited for Marshall to look up and as soon as he did she smiled at them both. With as much grace and poise as possible she shifted the plate of blueberry pie in her hand and slammed it into Kandi's face. Just for emphasis she turned the plate to the right and then the left for maximum smearage.

"Oh, dear. Bless my heart, I'm so clumsy. Can you believe I just tripped?" Katelyn batted her eyelashes and flashed her oops pose from her modeling repertoire. It was so overdone that no one could believe her apology or had any doubt that this was the furthest thing from an accident as possible.

The café was silent. Everyone was leaning closer to make sure they didn't miss a word. They had to make sure they memorized every detail for the recounting they were all going to give.

"Marshall! Arrest her!" Kandi sputtered as she used her fingers to wipe away the pie in her eyes.

Her face was purple and clumps of crust were hanging from her eyelashes and chin. A whole blueberry was sitting on the end of her nose trying to decide if it wanted to slide off or not. A big blob of pie sat on her white shirt right in-between her overblown breasts.

"For what? Tripping? While the incident is unfortunate, it's not illegal." Marshall just smiled and sat back in the booth with one arm draped over the divider and the other resting on the table. Katelyn had the distinct impression he was enjoying himself.

"Judge! Do something! This was assault and battery. Attempted murder! That's it. She tried to kill me!"

"I'm sorry *Mrs.* Rawlings, I didn't see anything. And in all my years on the bench I've never seen or read about death by pie. I believe you're safe and you can rest assured that no laws have been broken."

But... but, I'm covered in pie and that bitch is the reason!

ɹeone must've seen something! Not all of you could have missed

Kandi screamed and looked around the café where suddenly

veryone was very occupied with their dinner. With a cry of dismay Kandi grabbed her big bag and held her purple face up as high as she could and stormed out of the café.

"So," Marshall drawled in his deep voice, "does this mean you'll go out with me now?"

Marshall grabbed his clipboard and looked over the names of the people who had shown up at the Wyatt's house. Mr. and Mrs. Wyatt were entertaining the volunteers along with his deputies. Well, really baby Sienna was entertaining them all as her grandmother Betsy held her. Will and Kenna were standing nearby talking to Cade, Cole, Paige, Dani, Mo and Ahmed. Miles and Pierce were talking to Henry and Tammy, Henry's young secretary. She was trying real hard to not look at Pierce.

The Rose sisters were helping Mrs. Wyatt put together little baskets for each pair of volunteers. Sheriff Nuggett was organizing a similar gathering in his county. When they had driven around the counties they had narrowed down the list of suspects to ten people. Six in Nuggett's county and four in Marshall's. They were really only going on a hunch. But, when they looked at the maps, visited the areas and read the criminal reports for people in those areas these four really stood out.

There was a husband and wife who had each served short stints in rehab for drugs. They also had a criminal neglect case that was tossed out when they handed the dog in question over to the humane society. The other suspects were men in their mid to late twenties with a history of violence toward animals. One had drowned a puppy and one had paid a fine and served three days in jail for beating his dog with his crutch. The others had been found guilty of

various charges of cruelty to animals. In most of the cases, a ne
saw something and reported it.

Nuggett and his men were going to be searching the woods in
county while Marshall and his group of volunteers were to patrol tr
private farms that sat on the county line. He wasn't thrilled with
using volunteers, but he didn't have the manpower that Nuggett
had. Keeneston was too small to afford much more than what they
had. However, he had devised a plan to have a law-enforcement
official with every group.

First, the Wyatts and the Roses were to stay at the house and wait
for reports from each section. They had a giant map and would take
notes on activities in each area. Cade and Annie would be in one
group. Will, Kenna, and Noodle would be in another. Cole and Paige
were in the third group. Miles, although not in law enforcement, was
going to take Pierce out in the fourth group. Ahmed, Dani, and Mo
would be in the fifth. Dinky, Tammy and Henry would be in the
sixth, and he and Katelyn would be in the final group.

He was expecting surveillance from them. They'd drive to the
farms and then find a good place to stake out. If they saw anything,
anything at all, they were to stay hidden and radio in immediately.

"Well, this is an interesting first date." Marshall turned and
found Katelyn standing behind him in tight black jeans, boots, and a
black t-shirt.

"I wanted you to remember it. But, I also had a C.I. tell me he
heard rumors of a fight tonight. He's not involved in them, so he
didn't get a text telling him where it was going to be held. These
things are done so secretly that if you're not in the group, it's hard to
find out the time or location."

"Hence the groups. When do we get going?" she asked.

He was lucky she was so understanding. Just a couple weeks ago,
he would've sworn that she'd stomp her foot and leave him high and
dry for not taking her to a five-star restaurant for their first date. But,
he was starting to get to know her and he liked what he was finding.

kay! Listen up! Annie, Dinky, Noodle, Cole, Ahmed, and Miles e group leaders. They have the maps showing where you're to nd where everyone else is. Everyone should have a radio. If you n't, let Beauford know and he'll get you one. The goal is to canvas ne section of farm you're assigned to. Stay quiet and hidden. If you hear anything, don't approach. Stay where you are and call it in.

"From what I've learned, most of these fights take place late, around midnight. So, don't be surprised if you don't see or hear anything right away as it's only ten o'clock now. But, you may stumble upon them getting set up, which is what I'm hoping. We'll all meet back here at three. It's going to be a late night. The Rose sisters and Mrs. Wyatt are going to stay here and make coffee. Feel free to come back for a break and to refill whenever you need to."

Marshall thanked the group and waited for them to head out before taking Katelyn to his cruiser.

"I'm sorry I couldn't take you out to a nice restaurant or something."

"It's okay. Getting these guys will be the best date ever." She smiled as she slid into her seat.

He sure hoped it would be.

Chapter Twelve

Marshall scanned the area again and set down his binoculars. Nothing. Just like there was the last hour. It was one in the morning and they had covered every inch of the Wyatt property. No one else had found anything yet either. Ahmed had just phoned in and said they were still searching Mo's property, but hadn't found anything yet. Ahmed's group and Annie and Cade were the only ones still covering new ground. The others had searched and found what they thought were good spots and were hunkered down waiting and listening.

"I think this would be a good spot. It's quite a distance away from where we found Alice and we can even park the cruiser behind those bushes over there," he told Katelyn as he drove the car to a row of honeysuckles.

"It seems so late. I don't think anything is going to happen."

"I don't know whether to be happy or sad about that. I'd have sworn tonight was the night." Marshall turned the engine off and looked around.

The night was quiet and the full moon was large in the sky. Crickets chirped and the sounds of small animals scampering through the woods reached his ears. He turned his head and stole a glance at Katelyn as she scanned the trees for movement. The moonlight made her blonde hair seem silver and cast a glow around her. She was simply breathtaking.

n kept her head turned away from Marshall as much as she
.. He was dressed in camouflage cargo pants with a gun
ched to his hip and another one strapped to his thigh. His khaki t-
irt was stretched tight across his chest making it hard to focus on
he task at hand.

They had talked almost constantly the past couple of hours. She
had laughed at his childhood stories of growing up with five
brothers and how they tortured their sister only to be tortured by her
when she became a teenager and started bringing boys home.

She had been warmed by his obvious love of his family and told
him of the dress up she used to play in her grandmother's closet with
her hats and gloves. She told him about working her way through
school and some of the scandals she had seen when she had been
working as a model.

They had laughed and shared funny stories and some not so
funny ones. She had never really confided in many people and was
surprised to find how easy it was to talk to him. He didn't judge her
like she thought he would and he listened to every word she said,
tossing in sarcastic remarks here and there that had her giggling.

"Katelyn," she heard his husky voice and turned to him. "You're
so beautiful, inside and out."

She felt his hand cup her cheek. She closed her eyes and gave
way to the feeling. She had been yearning for his touch and he was
finally giving it to her.

"I'm so glad you came out with me tonight. I like being with you.
You draw me in and I find it hard to control myself." His voice was
now a gravely whisper. He pulled her face towards his and brought
his lips down on hers. A storm of passion arose within her the
moment his lips met hers. She slid her hands under his shirt and felt
the rippling of his muscles. He pulled her closer to him as he ripped
her shirt from her pants and brought it over her head.

His hands cupped her breasts through her black lace bra until she
pushed him back and hopped over the laptop computer and radio
and straddled him. Her bottom was pressed against the steering

wheel, but she didn't notice as she stripped off his shirt and ran her hands over his chest.

She kissed him hard and felt his pleasure rise. She kissed her way down to his neck as his hands moved to caress her breasts. The feelings were so intense she couldn't see anything but stars and couldn't hear anything except for their heavy breathing.

"Katelyn!"

"Hmm?" She moaned as she sucked on his earlobe.

"The radio is going off." Dammit.

Marshall groaned and reached around her and turned up the radio to hear who was reporting in. Could they just once not be interrupted?

"Shots fired! I repeat shots fired!" Marshall heard Cade yell. "Annie! Get your ass back here!"

Marshall felt Katelyn sit straight up, hitting her head against the roof of the car in her haste to get back to her seat. He grabbed the radio and pressed the button down.

"Cade, what's going on?" He had already turned on the car and was hitting the gas pedal as he repeated his question, but got only static in return.

"Oh God. Are they okay? Annie's pregnant," Katelyn's voice escalated as she got more scared.

"I know she is. Annie is a tough woman, but a smart one. And don't underestimate Cade. He'll take care of her."

But, he didn't want to leave it all to Cade. His brother would kill him if something happened to Annie or the baby. He pressed the accelerator down as the car kicked up dirt and flew over the small hills and through the pastures of the Wyatt farm heading to the county land Cade and Annie were patrolling.

Katelyn was holding on tight as Marshall gunned the car. She had barely gotten on her shirt and zipped up her pants when they flew through an open gate onto the county land.

"Marshall! There!"

Katelyn pointed to the woods as two figures turned directions
nd ran deeper into the trees when they saw the lights from the car.
Marshall slid the car to a stop and had the door open in one move.

"Stay," was all he said before he took off into the darkness.

"Yea right!" Katelyn yelled to him as she chased after the figures.

She may not have his stealth as he wound his way through the
woods, but she had endurance. She had been a runner since she was
a kid.

"What the hell do you think you're doing? Get your ass back in
the car!" Marshall yelled over his shoulder at her.

"That didn't work for your brother, do you think it'll work for
you?"

Katelyn couldn't see very far past Marshall, but the sound of the
two people running was still near. Suddenly the roar of an engine
broke into the night. It revved and then took off into the woods.
Marshall sped up and left her far behind as he chased after the
taillights.

"Son of a bitch!" She heard him yell somewhere nearby.

Katelyn was in good shape, she knew she was, but they must've
covered a mile in under seven minutes. She was bent at the waist
dragging in deep breaths of air when she heard Marshall approach.

"Well, it wasn't a total loss. There's a house back there where the
ATV was parked. Maybe it has some evidence in it."

"You're not even breathing hard," she accused.

She saw the moon reflect off of his white teeth as he flashed her a
smile and went to check out the dark house.

"I'm pretty sure we're over the county line. I better call Nuggett
and let him know where we are."

Marshall pulled out his phone and made the call as he walked the
perimeter of the property. He closed the phone and bent down to
pick up a spiked collar. He held it up for her to see.

"Looks like there have been some dogs here."

Katelyn stepped from the tree line to take a look. Upon closer
inspection the house was in a state of abandonment, not residency.

Old rusty cages lined the back of the house, hidden under a tarp. Cages weren't evidence of fighting, and neither was a spiked collar, but it was just too curious.

"Can we look inside?" she asked.

"Yes. This is all public land."

With gun drawn, Marshall went in first and did a sweep of the house. She waited outside listening to every sound and trying to figure out if it was an animal or if the people were coming back. She had a sudden urge to jump behind Marshall and cling to him. She was just overreacting she told herself.

"It's all clear. I found a room full of dog-fighting paraphernalia."

He led her through the house to a room off the back that held some more cages, riding crops, pinch collars, and cattle prods. Katelyn shuddered at the thought of what these were used for. She waited by the door as Marshall took photos with his phone before heading into a small room with a bed.

"They must sleep here after fights," Marshall said more to himself than to her.

There were candy wrappers and bags of chips tossed around the room. A worn blanket and two thin pillows where strewn haphazardly on a small double bed. The place was filthy, but there didn't seem to be any leaks or pests so the house must be somewhat taken care of.

"Why is there a house out here in the woods on county property?" she asked as she opened the closet door.

"This property sits on both counties. It used to be a farm, but the owners died decades ago. There was no will and there were no heirs to be found. The property fell into neglect during the search and fell behind in taxes. In the end the counties took control over it."

"Why wasn't it sold?"

"There was always someone on city council in Keeneston and over to Lipston that blocked the vote. They claim it's good to keep it for a park, even though only the main house is used for a park, the other 400 plus acres are just trees and open fields that are left for life. There's this house and two other smaller ones that have en left sitting here empty."

Katelyn stepped back and looked at the bed again. Was she crazy or was there something under there?

"What?"

"I think there's a big box under the bed, but I'm not really inclined to see what else is under that bed." The wood boards were worn and there were obvious holes in the foundation. While she didn't see any rats, she was so not taking the chance.

Marshall aimed his flashlight towards the bed and saw the end of a box peeking out from under the burnt orange blanket. He walked over to the bed and she followed close behind. He used his flashlight to move the blanket out of the way and then froze. Katelyn leaned around him and looked into the box and gasped.

"Is that dynamite?" she asked in a whisper, afraid any noise would set it off.

"A whole shit load. Because who doesn't keep dynamite under their bed? I mean, I know I do. Where do you keep yours?"

"With my shoes," she quipped. "This can't be safe."

"I guess as long as there's no spark or fire it won't go off."

Marshall bent down to look at the dynamite again when the old glass window shattered. A bullet whizzed right in front of Katelyn and right over Marshall's back.

"That's not good. Move!" he yelled.

She stood rooted to the spot looking at the bullet lodged in the wall just five feet away.

"I said, move it Blondie!"

He grabbed her arm and yanked hard. The pain finally shook her out of her trance. She let him pull her out the door as more shots started to pepper the room.

"Keep your head down!" he yelled back to her.

She lowered her head and followed him down the small hall and out the back door. He pulled her harder, and now out in the open farther away from the gunfire, she could focus more on running instead of getting shot. They made it to the tree line when the fir. charge went off and the back part of the house exploded into a thousand splintered pieces. The force pushed her forward and into the air. Marshall had his arms around her in a split second. The two of them crashed to the ground with her head cradled in his arms and her face in the grass. He covered her completely as debris from the old wooden house fell around them.

Heat from the massive explosion reached her as Marshall finally released his hold on her. They sat up and turned to look at what was left of the burning house. She looked around, not knowing if the ringing in her ears was sirens or an effect from the explosion. Flashing lights converged on them from every direction.

Annie, with a very pissed-off look on her face, was the first to reach them. Cade, with an equally pissed-off look, was right behind her.

"Are you two alright? Did you get them?"

"We're okay. And, no, they had too much of a head start on us. They got on an ATV and took off. I didn't think they'd come back to blow up the house, but I guess they were trying to get rid of all the evidence inside," Marshall answered.

"I'm sorry I didn't get them. I was so close. I even had an open shot, but *someone* thought I wasn't a good enough cop to take them down in my *delicate* condition and stopped me. It didn't matter I was wearing two vests and could've shot them from a very safe distance if I hadn't been prevented from doing so," Annie said through gritted teeth.

"He's right. You shouldn't have chased after them, not while you're pregnant," Marshall said as he got up.

"Don't you start too! I think I'm the only one here who can say what I can and cannot do, so don't pull that macho crap on me while you're standing there without your shirt on and while Katelyn's shirt is on inside out...and backwards. At least I was doing my job and not fooling around." Annie cringed and then looked to Katelyn, "Sorry."

atelyn felt her face flush as she looked down at her shirt. Oh
d, could this get any worse?

"I was doing my job. I was just passing time, and I did at least
manage to get some evidence," he said as he held up his phone.

Katelyn whipped her head up at the same time she heard Annie
suck in her breath. Passing time. That's what she was there for, to
pass the time.

"Now, *deputy*, I want my report. What the hell happened?"
Marshall hadn't even noticed the look she was giving him or the look
Annie was bestowing on both of them as some of the Lipston
deputies made their way over.

"I saw lights at the end of the county property, down by the
stream that connects to the Wyatt property. I stopped the car as soon
as I saw something and Cade was about to radio in when they
started shooting at the cruiser. They must have had sentries posted. I
told Cade to take cover and returned fire to the general area the shots
were coming from. It scared them and suddenly there were people
everywhere in the distance. Huge trucks, small cars… everyone was
starting their engines and taking off in the opposite direction. I was
losing all my evidence so I took off towards the action only to see
two people running like crazy with a large duffle bag. They appeared
not to have a car, so I took off after them until *someone* grabbed me."

"Excuse me, if ya'll don't mind my interruption. Passing time?
You were just passing time? I should've saved one stick of dynamite
to shove up…" Katelyn took a deep breath and looked into
Marshall's wide shocked eyes.

"I believe I've given my report and in my *delicate* condition I
better get home before I'm consumed with the vapors and faint dead
away. Katelyn, would you like a ride?" Annie asked with a forced
smile.

"I'd love one, thank you." Katelyn stepped forward and stood
next to Annie.

"I hate riding in the back of cop cars. It always makes me feel like
a criminal," Cade whined.

"I know," Annie smiled. "That's why you can get a ride home with your brother."

Annie pivoted on her heel and Katelyn followed suit. She might really need to get to know Annie better. She liked this feisty redhead more and more.

Katelyn and Annie didn't talk on the short walk back to the cruiser. She opened the car door and slid into the passenger seat. Maybe Annie would be nice enough to pull over so she could put her shirt on correctly.

"Katelyn, I'm so sorry about pointing out your shirt. I was just so angry and I totally didn't mean to embarrass you, but it came rushing out anyway. I am just so...so...so sorry," Annie said as she maneuvered the car onto the nearest dirt road.

"It's okay. I'd have said something too. Do you mind if I change my shirt real fast. My grandma has already walked in on us once. I don't want her to get any ideas that this is more serious than it is. Especially since it's over now."

Katelyn couldn't help the feeling of being crushed. Her heart felt as if it were being torn in half.

"Anyway, thanks for the lift home. I don't think I could've looked Marshall in the face again. It would hurt way too much right now."

"You're welcome. I thought I might shoot Cade if he went on any longer. He's under the belief that you become totally useless and unable to perform even the simplest daily functions when you're pregnant," Annie told her with a roll of her eyes that showed Katelyn she might be angry, but she loved him for it.

"At least Cade loves you. Marshall thinks I'm pretty useless overall, except for sex apparently. All the other times he just gives me this stern, unhappy look."

"I know that look well!" Annie laughed. "But, that's not the 'you're useless' look he's giving you."

"Then what is it?" Katelyn asked.

nat's the 'I love you, and must protect you look'. Cade has the look."

Katelyn laughed when Annie tried to impersonate Cade and arshall. But there was one problem.

"That's funny. But, Marshall doesn't love me. I think we all know after what he said what he thinks of me."

"I think it's because he can't express himself. These Davies men aren't too good at connecting to and then expressing their feelings. But, I guess it doesn't matter." Annie shrugged.

"Why not?"

"Do you really care? You've made it really clear by rejecting him so many times that you're only going out with him out of pity. I mean, you can only say no so many times, right?"

Katelyn was taken aback, "I don't know. It just seems like we're so drawn to each other, but a relationship can't be built on lust alone. I said no because I think he just wants to *pass time* and I don't want to let myself fall head over heels for someone who thinks of me as a booty call."

"And if he showed you that you weren't a booty call and that he cared for you?" Annie asked quietly as she pulled up to the Wyatt house.

"It would be a dream come true. I've never had a man in my life who actually cared for me. Thanks for the ride. I enjoyed talking to you."

Katelyn slumped her shoulders and went inside the old house. She picked up her phone and dialed.

"We have an issue and I have an idea. Let's gather at Dani's and make sure Ahmed is there."

A plan was formulating in her mind as she drove the short distance to Dani's farm. The front door opened then Paige and Dani stepped outside.

"Is Kenna here yet?"

"She's just feeding Sienna. That's probably her." Dani pointed t the headlights in the distance. "What's up?"

"I had an interesting talk with Katelyn I want to tell you all about."

"Gossip, it's what makes the world go round," Paige said as they watched Kenna get out of the car.

"What's this about? Is everyone okay? Ahmed didn't get picked up for weapons charges, did he?" Kenna asked as she hurried over to the group.

"No, he did not." Ahmed materialized out of the darkness to join them.

"Well, now that everyone is here, tell us what's going on," Paige said, her voice full of excitement.

Annie told them what happened in the woods and what Marshall said. The girls all hissed as Ahmed's jaw tightened. Then she told them about her conversation with her in the car and their outraged faces turned soft.

"So, what do you think Paige? You know them both the best."

"It's true. Katelyn has really only had Beauford and Ruth on her side. Shelly too. But, that's it. Most of the men who dated her just wanted to use her for one thing or another. But, I also know that Marshall wouldn't mess with a woman like Katelyn unless he really liked her. And she's definitely not someone he'd have a one-night stand with."

"Two," Ahmed said simply.

"Two what?" Paige asked.

"They've been together twice." Everyone looked around, shrugging in confusion.

"Would you care to elaborate?" Kenna asked.

"The night of Cade and Annie's wedding." All the women's mouths dropped open.

"That's who she went home with?"

"How do you know?"

Everyone tossed out questions until Ahmed held up a hand. "I have my sources. So, what's this idea you have?"

Annie outlined it and then looked right at Ahmed, "What do you think?"

"I like Katelyn. You all know we went out a couple of times. But, I have to agree with Paige. Marshall loves her and I'm pretty sure she loves him. I'll do it."

"Are you sure?" she asked.

"Yes. It would give me pleasure to see her happy. Marshall too. I respect and like them both. I would never stand in the way of their happiness."

"You're a good man, Ahmed," Dani told him.

"Maybe this will help make up for some of the dark things I have had to do in my life."

Before anyone could say anything, Ahmed walked off and disappeared into the darkness. Annie sniffled and Paige let loose with her tears.

"Enjoying pregnancy ladies?" Dani joked as she tried to wipe away a tear before they saw.

Kenna pulled out her cell phone and dialed a number.

"Bed and Breakfast," a tired voice mumbled.

"Gather the ladies, we have a mission."

Chapter Thirteen

Marshall was having the worst day imaginable. He'd been a horrible ass last night, well, early this morning, and Katelyn hadn't given him any chance to apologize. On top of that, he hadn't gone to bed yet, it was now five thirty at night, and things just kept getting worse.

He had tried to apologize at seven this morning when he finally wrapped up the scene at the demolished house and fighting area Annie had found. Mrs. Wyatt told him she was at work. Shelly wouldn't budge from the front door of the clinic. Bekah wouldn't move from the back either.

He was going to go home to take a quick nap when he got an emergency call and had to break up a fight at the PTA over reserving chairs for the concerts and plays the kids put on. Just when he was ready to go home again, he got called out to the farmers' market for a fight over a cut of pork being organic or not. Ironically, he then got called over to old man Tabby's farm to settle a dispute over a pig he had bought.

Now he was two miles from town and he'd blown a tire. All he wanted was a whole pitcher of Miss Violet's special sweet tea and for Miles or Pierce to get done with work so they could drive his sorry, soon to be drunk, ass home.

"That bitch ruined everything! I can't believe they found us. I knew nothing about this, I swear." She had never been so angry.

She had closed her books and grabbed whatever cash she could the second she heard the first shot. People had grabbed their money, dogs, guns, and drugs and hightailed it out the back of the park faster than she thought possible.

"You better do more than swear. You and your partner get paid to keep us informed. If you fail at that job, there's no reason to keep you around."

"Don't threaten me Watkins. I have information and I'll use it. Just remember that."

"Stop it you two. What are we going to do?" Camilla asked.

"We're criminals, aren't we? So let's go back to our roots and wreak a little havoc." Andre smiled and opened a large trunk that sat in the living room.

Katelyn's day sucked. She tossed and turned for the remaining hours of the night before getting a phone call at six from Bekah. A dog was hemorrhaging and needed emergency surgery. After a two-hour surgery, she started seeing her clients. Everyone was talking about last night too. They all wanted to know every detail. Somehow, luckily, Marshall's comments hadn't made the rounds yet.

"Katelyn?" Shelly poked her head into her office.

"What?"

"There was a phone call for you earlier."

"I told you, unless an animal was critical, push all phone calls to tomorrow."

"I know. That's why I went ahead and accepted it."

"Accepted what? You're not making any sense."

"It was Paige and she invited us to a girls' night dinner at the café tonight. Miss Violet is making us a special dessert dinner. Nothing but dessert and her special iced tea! Doesn't that sound perfect? And a table of girls to help ward off all gossipers who want a reenactment of last night. So, I'm your driver for the night. Grab your purse, it's time to go."

"Shelly, I'm tired…"

"Hush. It's just what you need. Now move." Shelly used her best mom voice and Katelyn instinctively complied.

Within minutes she was walking into the café with Shelly leading the way. Miss Daisy had put together two square tables for Shelly, Dani, Paige, Kenna, Annie, and herself.

"Katelyn! I'm so glad you two came!" Paige got up and gave them both a hug. "We're going to have so much fun!"

"Hi everyone." Katelyn smiled and sat down in an empty chair.

"Here you go hon, turtle brownie and a glass of special iced tea." Miss Daisy set both in front of her.

Carmel oozed over the dark chocolate brownie with walnuts, whipped cream, and a cherry on it. It was heaven.

"Thank you. This is just what I needed."

Conversation flowed and after a couple glasses of iced tea, Katelyn finally managed to laugh along with the stories the girls were telling. Dani was trying her best to do an impersonation of her father-in-law and her mother-in-law demanding she have a baby. She wasn't getting any younger after all!

Katelyn's laughter stopped in her throat. She guessed she'd known she'd have to see him again, she was just hoping it wasn't so soon. She watched as Marshall made his way to the table.

"Hello ladies." He looked horrible. Good. "I just wanted to say have a good evening." He tried to smile and then walked to his usual booth.

He didn't even look at her. He also didn't try to apologize. Yup, she'd been an idiot. He was only using her as his booty call. Next time he came around she'd send him packing in no uncertain terms.

"Ahmed!" Dani shouted as she raised her glass. "To Ahmed!"

The girls cheered and took a drink as he made his way to the table smiling. She felt the room raise ten degrees as all the women melted.

"Ladies," he said in a soft accented voice that caused Shelly to fan herself.

Ahmed kissed Dani on the cheek, then Kenna, Paige, Annie, and Shelly. Katelyn found herself laughing at the glazed look on her friend's face.

"Katelyn." Was it just her, or was his voice much lower and husky?

"Hi Ahmed," she smiled up to him.

She tilted her head up and tapped her cheek with her finger teasingly. She was grinning and looking at Annie's laughing face when she felt his finger under her chin. She turned her eyes to his and in that split second saw his lips descending onto hers. He pulled her up against him and kissed her hard. Katelyn's mouth only opened because she was so shocked and he took full advantage moving his tongue into her mouth.

He was there, with her pressed against his body and then he was gone. She opened her eyes right in time to see Marshall's fist connect with Ahmed's face. Marshall looked at her shocked face and then turned and walked toward the door.

"Dammit! A man can only take so much," he mumbled before disappearing out the door.

Katelyn still hadn't closed her mouth and she certainly couldn't say anything. In fact no one could. The whole café sat in silence and watched the door slam. In unison, they all turned to where Ahmed sat on the floor with an already swollen black eye.

"Well," Miss Lily said from her seat by her neighbor Edith, "I do believe Ruth can book the church now."

"Uh-huh, that's a man in love right there," Miss Daisy announced.

"That was just the most romantic thing I ever saw," Tammy sighed.

The café agreed as Tammy hurried to help Ahmed up. He smiled at her and gave Katelyn a wink with his good eye before heading out the door himself.

What in the hell just happened? He felt like he had been asking himself that a lot recently. One second he was sitting at the table having a drink by himself and the next he punched his friend right in the face. Not just any friend either. No, he had to go knock the one guy who had the ability to kill him in his sleep. Then the SOB had smiled. He had actually smiled at Marshall from his place on the ground right after he hit him.

He couldn't help it though. He had seen Ahmed come in and didn't pay any attention to him giving the girls a kiss on the cheek, but his kiss with Katelyn started a reaction that was intense and immediate. No one was allowed to kiss the woman he loved. Marshall stopped in his tracks.

"Oh God, I love her."

Katelyn sat down and finally closed her mouth. What just happened? Why did Ahmed kiss her? Why did Marshall punch him? Okay, okay. Marshall didn't look at her when he came in. So, he doesn't care about her. But, Ahmed kissed her and he lost it. But, he wouldn't lose it if he didn't care about her. And Ahmed — they had already tried dating and kissing, and it didn't work. He was a fabulous kisser, no doubt about it, but it lacked the spark that was there when she and Marshall kissed.

Katelyn tuned out the noise as her mind raced trying to connect all the dots. Did Ahmed kiss her then to see what Marshall would do? And when he punched Ahmed it meant… it meant what? Oh.My.God. Katelyn bolted up from her chair.

"He loves me," she said in wonder.

"You're just now getting that?" Miss Lily asked.

"And you're still here?" Annie laughed.

Katelyn grabbed her bag and Paige tossed her the keys to her truck.

"He'll probably be at the far pasture behind his house. He always goes there to think. Go to his house, take the dirt road to the left of the house back about a mile. His spot is at the top of the big hill at the end of the dirt road.

"Bless your heart, what are you waiting for?" Miss Daisy shooed her out the door to the clapping of the patrons.

Marshall took another drink of beer and looked up at the stars in the black night sky. His favorite thing about being so far out in the country was the night sky. No city lights to hide the stars. The only noise was that of the cows moving about the pasture below, the crickets chirping, and the sound of him kicking himself.

He should've never punched Ahmed. He was sure someone as classy and worldly as Katelyn would have found it offensive. He was going to have to apologize to her and to Ahmed both. There had to be some way to put her out of his mind. She had clearly chosen Ahmed and he needed to relinquish the field to him, no matter how much it hurt. Even worse, he had to find a way to be happy for them both.

He laid down on the grass and looked up at the rounded sky. What was he going to do? He listened to the breeze rustling the leaves and tried not to think about Katelyn. The sound of an engine interrupted his not thinking. He sat up and prepared to face the music. It was probably Miles coming to see what had happened. Miles was always the one who came to clean up any messes or to rescue them when they were overseas.

Marshall stood up and looked down at the headlights. They were from a pickup truck, so it couldn't be Miles or Cade. That left Pierce and Paige. Out of those two, he suspected it was Paige coming to yell at him. Just what he needed.

Well, if he was going to be yelled at, she could just climb the big ass hill and meet him up there. He smiled knowing that it would tick off his sister having to walk the short distance to the bottom of the hill and then all the way up it. It was the little things in life.

He watched Paige park and sat back down to wait the five minutes or so it would take her to reach him. The door opened and she got out of the car. Marshall squinted and then his eyes opened wide. Blonde hair shimmered in the moonlight and those long legs were certainly not his sister's. What was Katelyn doing here? He didn't know, but he was going to find out.

Chapter Fourteen

Marshall watched as Katelyn looked up the hill and then started walking the short distance to the bottom of the hill. She was halfway to the base when the sound of a rifle exploded through the night air from the tree line two hundred yards away from the path.

He watched in horror as Katelyn grabbed her stomach and fell to the ground as another round was fired. He felt his heart stop in his chest as he focused on Katelyn's body in the dirt. All his years of training took over and he was racing down the hill, zigzagging as he went to avoid the rifle fire.

His hand went automatically to his waist, but he wasn't in war and he wasn't on duty so the gun that had been a staple for so many years was locked up at home. Damn, he was totally defenseless, but that didn't stop him from pounding his way down the hill at breakneck speed.

Bullets hit the ground near him, spewing up dirt. He didn't look at them. He just kept his eyes on Katelyn. Both relief and fear flooded through him when he saw her move and slowly start crawling for the safety of the truck.

He was halfway down the hill when he lost his footing. He slipped on the dewy grass and felt his leg go out from under him. He landed hard on his hip and grimaced as he slid a few feet until he hit a rock. He was able to get his feet under him again and suck in another breath of air. He couldn't remember if he had been breathing or not.

At the bottom of the hill the firing stopped. By his count the gun held ten rounds. He figured he had less than five seconds before a new magazine was put into the rifle. He stopped zigzagging and sprinted straight for Katelyn. He slid next to her as if he was stealing a base in baseball. The sight of blood on her shirt was like a dagger to his heart.

"Are you okay?" Bullets dug into the ground as the shooter peppered them with a new magazine.

"Yes. It's just a scrape." Katelyn pulled herself another couple of feet before resting again.

"Good. Then this is going to hurt."

Marshall scooped her up into his arms and ran for all he was worth. He heard her groan as he pulled her close to his chest. He ran at an angle, keeping his back towards the tree line so any bullets would hit him and not her. He bent down to hide behind the truck for cover.

"I'm going to put you on the bench behind the seat. I have to put you down for a second, alright?"

Katelyn nodded as she bit her lip. She didn't want to worry him. He was so focused on getting her to safety. She couldn't believe it when the first gunshot rang out. She actually didn't know what to do. She just stood there, confused, until the second shot hit her. She had looked at it, and it was bleeding, but it didn't look serious. However, it sure hurt like the dickens.

She had tried to make it to the car for shelter, but she had looked back when the gunshots moved away from her and focused instead on the hill. She had seen Marshall, racing down the hill like a man possessed. She had a hard time remembering she even knew him. His face was set in such a focused and serious way that he was almost unrecognizable. He had moved with such speed and agility that she could only stare. He was an action hero right out of a movie. An action hero who was now placing her across the backbench and giving her orders. Too bad she didn't hear them. She had a feeling though, that it didn't matter. He'd do anything to keep her safe and she trusted him to do so.

Marshall pushed back the passenger seat and felt better knowing he had Katelyn safe. He climbed over the seat and the center stick shift and into the driver's seat. He turned the key and a new round of shots shattered the windshield. He ducked down and checked on Katelyn. She was going to be fine. He had looked at her wound when he laid her down. It was bleeding, but it wasn't bad. Katelyn, not used to being shot, was starting to show signs of shock.

He shifted the car into reverse and floored the pedal. The truck rocketed backwards, kicking up dust as he spun the wheel hard while shifting into drive. As soon as he was out of range of the rifle, he bent down and grabbed Katelyn's purse. Why did she need such a large purse? He gave up feeling around for her cell phone and dumped the contents onto the passenger seat. He pushed aside keys, a stethoscope, a small bag of Kleenex, something he didn't know what it was or could possibly be used for, and then finally found the cell phone. He dialed 9-1-1 and waited for the overnight dispatch to pick up.

"Keeneston 9-1-1, how can I help you dear?"

"It's me. Shots have been fired on my farm. Katelyn's been hit. I'm taking her to the ER in Lexington right now."

"Sheriff! Oh thank the stars! We've been trying to get hold of you for an hour. Noodle was doing some night fishing when he was shot!"

"Is he alive?" This couldn't be happening?

"Yes. He was out in the lake over by Lipston when he heard the sound of the gun cocking. He said the person who shot at him was about 50 yards away behind some cover on the other side of the cove he was in. Anyway, he heard the gun cock and then dove underwater. The bullet hit his leg instead of his chest. He stayed underwater as long as he could and came up for air some distance away. Then he made his way back to his car and drove to UK's hospital."

"Thank God he's okay. I think Katelyn will be fine too. The wound isn't bad, but she's in shock. Call Sheriff Nuggett and see if he'll come out with some of his men to help secure the crime scene. See if you can send someone to my farm until I can get there. If you can't find anyone, call one of my brothers."

"Will do. I just don't understand it, not at all. Why shoot two unarmed people?"

"I don't know, but I'll find out."

Marshall pulled up to the emergency room at the University of Kentucky Hospital and flagged a nurse sneaking a smoke before running inside to get a wheelchair. She was back with a doctor and a stretcher before he had even gotten Katelyn out of the back seat. She had stopped shaking, but was still glassy eyed.

He told the doctor what had happened and all the medical information he knew about her. That just made him feel worse. He didn't know her blood type and he didn't know if she was allergic to anything, he felt totally helpless.

"Marshall!"

"Annie, Dinky, what are you all doing here?"

"Dispatch called an hour ago and told us about Noodle, so we came here to check on him. Sherriff Nuggett already called me and told us he's on his way to interview Noodle."

"He's going to be fine. But, was that Katelyn? What's going on?" Annie asked as she looked towards the big doors Katelyn had just gone through.

"Yes. She came to see me on the farm and when she got out of the car she was shot. As soon as I started running toward her, the gunfire was directed at me. She was wounded, but it really was more of a bad gash. She started to go into shock though so I rushed her here."

"Why is someone shooting at the police?" Dinky asked.

"I don't know, but I'm going to say something right now that both of you won't like. First, if either of you go outside, I want your flak vests on. Second, Annie, I want you inside until we catch this person. I will not risk you or your baby getting shot."

"Okay."

"What?"

"Okay. I'll go from home to work and that's it." Annie's lips were pursed and Marshall knew that her maternal instincts just overrode her instinct to go after the bad guys.

"I'll pick you up and drive you to work," Dinky told her.

"Thank you. Good, here's Sheriff Nuggett. If I can't be out there to shoot the bastard, at least I can try to figure out what's going on." Annie gave a quick head nod to Nuggett as he came toward them.

"I'm sorry about your man, Davies. How is he?"

"We think he'll be fine. Did you find anything at the crime scene?" Marshall asked.

"Yes. We found the casings and a couple of muffin wrappers. Never found those at a crime scene before," Nuggett told him as he scratched his head. "Banana nut. I wonder if it means something."

Banana nut muffins... why was that bothering him? Something was nagging him from the back of his mind, but he just couldn't put a finger on it.

"Marshall! How's my baby?" He looked at the emergency room door and found Mr. and Mrs. Wyatt hurrying in with Miss Lily right on their heels.

"We haven't heard yet, but it didn't look too serious."

"Oh, thank God!" Marshall watched as Beauford put his arm around his wife and gave her a supportive squeeze.

Within minutes the hospital waiting room filled up with his friends and family. They milled around for an hour before the doors to the ER opened and Dr. Francis came out with two nurses pushing Katelyn and Noodle in wheelchairs. Katelyn was now wearing scrubs and looked stiff. Noodle had a big grin on his face and wide white gauze wrapped around his upper leg, sticking out of his jeans that had been cut off into very short jorts.

Mr. and Mrs. Wyatt rushed to Katelyn's side and Marshall found himself frozen to the spot just so thankful she was there. He knew it wasn't a bad injury, but that didn't mean his heart hadn't been painfully pinched until he could see her again and know she was fine.

"Well, Ms. Jacks was grazed on her left side. Took about five stitches to close up, but she's good to go. Just try not to stretch those stiches. Mr. Miller was shot through his thigh. He's going to need to stay off the leg for a couple of days and no active duty for at least three weeks and not until he's cleared by a doctor."

"Thank you, doctor. I'll take Eugene home with me and make sure he's well taken care of until he's able to be up and about on his own," Miss Lily said as she came to stand next to Noodle.

Noodle looked up at Dr. Francis with a longing look and Dr. Francis shrugged, her shoulders hitting her curly brown hair. Everyone noticed the look that passed between them and Marshall looked back at Noodle. His deputy was totally enamored with the pretty little doctor. And from the looks of things, the feeling was mutual.

"Oh no you don't, young man! Not while you're recuperating!" Miss Lily grabbed the wheelchair and started pushing him out the door lecturing him on thinking about "that" while shot up and in a wheelchair. Poor Dr. Francis turned bright red and looked completely mortified.

"Don't worry, she does that to everyone," Kenna told her.

"Yeah, I got hit with a broom for kissing on her patio," Will smiled.

"Eugene? I didn't know that was his name. No wonder he goes by Noodle."

"Shut up Pierce," Marshall groaned.

His younger brother just smiled and rocked back on his heels. He winked at Dr. Francis and made her blush a deeper red. His brother was always the smart-ass and always an instigator, but he was usually more tuned into people's emotions and should've known he was embarrassing the poor doctor.

Before Marshall could tell Pierce to apologize, he gave the doctor another wink and she laughed. Well, maybe his brother was growing up after all. He felt a tap on his shoulder and turned around to see Mr. Wyatt in a state. Oh crap. Beauford was known for being cutthroat in business and now he was staring at him with narrowed eyes.

"I told you to woo her, not get her shot!"

"Papa!" Katelyn gasped.

"Sir, you're right. It's all my fault. I should've heard him creeping up and loading his weapon." Without realizing it, Marshall had moved to stand at attention in front of Beauford.

"Beauford, you apologize to this nice young man right now. Can't you see he's already punishing himself? His face is pale and he has practically broken his hand by squeezing his fist so hard."

Marshall watched as Beauford gave him a lookover and then with a nod he turned to his granddaughter. He had been forgiven.

"Now darlin', how are you feeling?" He asked her.

"I'm okay Papa. I'm just very sore and very tired. I think the pain medication they gave me is putting me to sleep."

"Let's get you home and I'll give you one of my guns to take out with you to keep safe."

"No thanks. You know I don't like guns."

"Then you should take Alice with you for protection whenever you go out."

"I have Ruffles. I'll start taking her."

"Sugar, that dog is nothing but fluff and bows. She's a spoiled poodle princess and doesn't know the first thing about protection. Take both of the girls with you. They are practically inseparable now anyway."

"I will, Papa. I just don't understand why they shot at Noodle and me. Why were we targeted?"

"She's right," Dinky said. "Maybe we need to put the dog-fighting investigation on hold and find out who's taking potshots at innocent people. A shooter at large is far more dangerous."

Will took a step forward, his tall frame overshadowing Dinky's smaller one. "This just seems pretty coincidental to me."

"I was thinking the same thing, honey," Kenna said as her brows creased in thought. "It's like they're trying to throw you off track."

"So, what we have is an unfinished fight and a distraction," Cole said as he took off his black cowboy hat and ran his fingers through his black hair. His silver eyes narrowed as Marshall could see him fitting the puzzle pieces together, the same puzzle pieces he had just put together.

"A distraction from something even bigger. They just had their big fight busted by Annie and now they have to redeem themselves in the eyes of the community before the community will bring them back in," Marshall explained.

"No one would show if they tried to hold another match. They have no credibility now. But by shooting a deputy and a veterinarian who was helping with the investigation, they not only had you looking in another direction, they also earned back respect. That was very clever," Mo said, almost more to himself than to the crowd gathered.

"This means they'll try to stage another fight soon to make up for the one we busted. I also think this next fight will be bigger and probably more dangerous. They'll want to put it all out there to make up for the last fight," Marshall told them.

"But... this is good for us." Annie nibbled on her lip as she thought.

"How so?" Mo asked.

"They think we're distracted. Let's use that to our advantage. We don't talk to anyone else about dog fighting. Only this small group will know what's really going on."

"What is really going on?" Dani looked confused as she tried to guess Annie's game plan.

"We use the shooting as a way to interview and look into people. We can go door to door and tell them we're looking for people who saw anything the night of the shooting. We get to peek in doors, especially the doors of the people we're already watching. But, we only talk of the shooting. We ask them for help and we never mention dog fighting again," Annie explained.

"That could work." Sheriff Nuggett looked to Marshall who nodded. Annie was onto something.

"Good work, Annie. I want you running point from the office with one of Nuggett's men. You'll tell us where to go, marking the questionable houses then tracking what we find," Marshall instructed. "It'll be slow going, but hopefully they'll think we're so preoccupied that they'll get a little sloppy."

"It sounds like you all have this well in hand. Come on Sweet Pea, let's get our girl home."

Before Marshall could stop them, Mr. and Mrs. Wyatt swept Katelyn out of the hospital and into the waiting car. Damn. He wanted — no he needed a chance to talk to Katelyn. If she had made it to the top of the hill tonight, he'd have told her he loved her and that he couldn't imagine living without her. Now all he could think about was telling her. If he could get her alone that is.

Chapter Fifteen

arshall felt like a teenager as he darted behind trees and made his way to the back of Wyatt Estate. He had talked with the group at the hospital a little longer and they had a plan to start looking into people tomorrow morning.

When they had finished, he went home and let his voicemail pick up the steady stream of calls looking for gossip. He had watched a SportsCenter rerun and even talked with Miles for a while. His brother was getting home later and later. Miles stopped by at three in the morning, still dressed in his suit, and was just now getting home. They had a beer and talked about the shooting and the game plan, which Miles agreed was a good course of action.

Marshall had drifted off to sleep somewhere around four in the morning and woke up just an hour later with thoughts of Katelyn. He was so worried about her. All he could imagine was her lying alone in her room in pain. He had to go to her. He *had* to tell her he loved her and he *had* to take care of her. And so at five thirty he was sneaking into Wyatt Estate.

He made it around the back of the house and saw a small light in Katelyn's bedroom. He hoped that meant she was awake, but then got worried that she wasn't sleeping. Dammit, what was happening to him? He was turning into his mother. He eyed the trellis full of purple morning glories and let out a breath. He was getting too old for this.

Putting his foot on the trellis, he pulled himself up slowly. He tried to avoid the flowers, just now opening for the day, as he made his way up to Katelyn's second-story window. Finally he reached the ledge. He peeked in and saw Katelyn asleep on her bed with Alice and Ruffles lying next to her. He tried the window, but it didn't open. He pulled out his army knife and wedged it under the lock. With a little jiggling the lock moved and he was able to push the window open.

He grabbed the ledge and pulled himself through. As soon as his first foot hit the ground he heard the growl. Looking up he saw and felt Ruffles with a mouthful of jeans. Alice stood slightly back and displayed a very impressive array of teeth.

"Shh. It's okay. It's just me."

The dogs growled louder and Alice took a step forward. Ruffles shook her head and his pants pulled at him as she tried her best to rip them. What was it with this dog and wanting his pants?

"Katelyn!" he whispered loudly. "Katelyn, help me." He saw her move a little in bed, so he tried again.

"Katelyn, your dog is eating me and your other dog is licking her chops. Come on Katelyn, I need you to wake up, honey."

Katelyn rolled over in bed and slowly opened her eyes. They fluttered and then shot open as she saw him backed up against the open window with her big white standard poodle viciously shaking his pant leg and little Alice standing stock still with her hair raised.

"Ruffles, Alice, it's okay. Time to go outside. It's okay. He's a friend."

Alice relaxed and reluctantly Ruffles gave up shaking his pant leg. With a look that could only be described as utmost diva, Ruffles tossed her head and headed out the cracked door and down the stairs.

She watched as Marshall went over to the door and quietly shut it. He turned back to her and gave her a shaky smile.

"What are you doing here?" she whispered.

"I didn't get any time to see you at the hospital and I had to make sure you were okay." He came over and sat on her bed. "I'm so sorry, doc. I should've gotten to you sooner. I should've heard the man coming and prevented the whole damn thing. Are you in much pain?"

"No. Actually hardly any at all. The pain medication is helping a lot and makes me feel really good. Plus, it wasn't really that bad. The doctor called it a scrape. Makes me kind of embarrassed really," she laughed.

"Why should you feel embarrassed?"

"Because I totally froze over a scrape. It's just because I've never been shot before."

"It's not as bad the second time," he joked.

She felt her eyebrows shoot up as she remembered she was talking to an Army veteran. Had he ever been injured while on duty?

"Have you ever been shot?"

"Yeah."

"How many times?" He was so nonchalant about it!

"Three."

"Oh my gosh! I also bet when you were shot it was more than a scrape. Where were you shot?"

"Once on my shoulder, once through my thigh and once through my calf."

"How did it happen? If you don't mind me asking."

"No, I don't mind. I got the shoulder shot when I was rescuing an ambassador from a new terrorist group that popped up and was later overtaken by the Taliban. The thigh shot I got when I was trapped in a crossfire and dove for some cover in the mountains of Afghanistan, and the calf wound was just a ricochet off part of a Somalian pirate ship I was boarding to rescue some hostages."

"Wow. I had no idea you did those things. I just pictured you at some base in the desert patrolling or helping rebuild towns."

"No one knows what I was doing except for Miles and Cade. They are called classified missions for a reason." He smiled and gave her a wink.

She had to see them. She wanted to touch them. She couldn't believe how strong the man was sitting next to her. There was a whole side of him she had never seen before. That no one had really seen before except his brothers.

"Can I see them?" she asked.

"See what?"

"Your scars." She wanted to try to feel what he went through.

"If you want."

She watched as he lifted his shirt over his head, exposing his muscled abdomen and chest. She had seen him naked before, but never noticed the scars.

"There?" She traced the small round scar on his left shoulder.

"Yup. That was my first one."

"It looks like a vaccination mark."

"It was a .22, which is a pretty small caliber, but it still hurt."

He stood up and unbuttoned his jeans. He pulled them down and Katelyn forgot all about bullet wounds.

"Oh, yeah, sorry about that. I sleep naked and when I just couldn't stand not seeing you any more I just slipped on my jeans and didn't bother with underwear."

Katelyn didn't mind. She ran her fingers down his leg until she found the scar hidden among a smattering of dark hair. She ran her hands down further until she found another scar on his calf. She couldn't believe she hadn't noticed them before. But like now, there were other more eye-grabbing things about him to see.

She reached up from her seat on the bed and grabbed his hands. Slowly, she pulled him down until he was sitting next to her on the bed. Katelyn ran her hand over his scar again and slowly leaned forward to kiss it. His warm muscles tightened under her touch and she felt the rumble of a groan under her lips as she kissed her way across his jaw.

"Katelyn, as much as I want to do this, you're injured."

"I'm a doctor and I think this is the best medicine you can give me," she said as she lay back down on the bed.

Marshall looked down as her blonde hair spilled over her pink and black satin nightgown. One of the small straps had fallen off her shoulder and exposed the top of her breast.

"Kiss me," she whispered.

"Yes, ma'am."

How could he not? He moved up the bed and sat next to her. He looked down as her blue eyes sparkled up at him. He placed his hand by her shoulder and held his weight on it as he bent down and kissed her. It was magic. He always felt as if the world disappeared when he was with her. His body had recognized her long before his heart caught up.

He danced his fingers up the satin gown to cup her breast as he deepened his kiss. She arched underneath him and moaned into his mouth. He needed to tell her why he came here tonight. The words were clawing at his throat for release.

"Katelyn," he said, pulling away from her slightly so he could look down into her eyes. "I have to tell you something."

"Yes?"

"I..."

"For the love of all that is holy! Do you ever wear clothes in my house?"

Marshall jumped up at the sound of Mrs. Wyatt's voice. She stood in the doorway with a tray full of food and a medicine bottle. He was about to dive for his clothes when Katelyn tossed him his shirt and mumbled something about finding her own place. He was pretty sure this was karma for his younger years. At this rate, he'd never get to tell her that he loved her more than the breath in his body.

Katelyn was so happy to be at work. Her grandmother had taken care of her, meaning she hadn't let her move out of bed, for three days. She couldn't take it any longer and had returned to work on Wednesday. She was happy to be here, but was thankful tomorrow was Friday.

She was stiff and sore, and if she moved too fast her stiches really pulled. They were so tight right now as they pulled the skin together to heal. She also had to stop herself from scratching at them.

She hated to admit it, but all this gossip had been very good for business. Shelly had been answering phones and making appointments all day long. Now, the day was over and she was happy to get home and lay in bed, just as long as she didn't tell her grandma or she'd be stuck in bed for the next week.

Her car was parked outside the back door and as she climbed in she heard a horn honk. Looking in her rearview mirror she saw a very large pickup truck. The door opened and out jumped Marcy Davies. She looked so out of place in that truck. She was better situated for one of those wood-paneled station wagons from the early eighties.

"Yoo-hoo!" she called as she came over to her window. "I'm so glad I caught you. I was just on my way home and thought that I'd see if you wanted to come to family dinner this Sunday with your grandparents. Obviously we couldn't do it last week like we planned. I didn't know how you were feeling and wanted to make sure you'd be up for it."

"I'd love to."

"Oh wonderful!" Marcy clapped her hands and gave her a beaming smile. "See you at six on Sunday."

"Looking forward to it."

She rolled up her window and thought of what she'd have to do to bribe her grandmother to behave.

★　　★　　★

"Was that your phone again, Andre?" Camilla called as she stirred the pasta boiling on the stove.

"Yup. It's our contact. He said that it's been quiet all week. He said the sheriff and all the deputies are talking about the shooting and are worried about a shooter taking out random people. They've been going house to house and asking if anyone has seen anything. He said to not be surprised if they make their way here at some point."

"But what about the dogs?"

"It's no longer a priority. We did it babe!" He picked her up and swung her around their kitchen.

"Then it's on for Saturday?"

"Yes, eleven o'clock. And babe, to get the attention of International I've invited everyone."

"Everyone? Oh no, please tell me you didn't, Andre."

"It had to be done. We'll get a cut of the local drugs and weapons. But to get the big shots here I had to pay them a cut of our local profit. We'll come out with some, but not much. However, they have major sway with who gets onto the circuit."

"You know I don't like those guys."

"I know, but if we get into the circuit we'll have to deal with them anyway. Better to get to know them now and have them help us pave our way. But, that doesn't mean I trust them one bit. We need to be prepared to protect our turf. We're the big dogs now and we'll show everyone that nobody messes with us and lives to tell about it."

Chapter Sixteen

arshall laid his cards on the table and grinned like fool. He had three aces and a king.

"Take that losers!" he ribbed his brothers at their weekly poker game.

This week it was his turn to host. Bob was always excited to see his uncles and enjoyed the massive amounts of chips they fed him as he sat in the sixth chair at the table watching the action.

"Who knew having old Mrs. Wyatt seeing you naked all the time upped your game?" Cade joked as he turned over his pair of jacks.

"Yeah, I might have to do a little streaking before next week's game. You cleaned me out." Pierce tossed his cards down on the table in disgust.

"How do you all know about that? Please tell me that it's not all over town," he groaned.

"I heard it from Paige, who heard it from Miss Lily. She confirmed with Katelyn. She thought there was no way her suave brother could be caught with his pants down three times so she had it verified." Cade pushed back his chair and slid his plate of leftover nachos to Bob.

"I heard it from Mom, who heard it from the girl that does her hair. Apparently she got it from her sister who delivers the paper and she got it from Miss Lily's neighbor, Edith." Pierce tossed in a chip as he picked up his new cards.

"Well, I better get home now that I've lost all my money. I need to stop at the gas station and pick up a variety of chocolate or I might not make it to morning," Cole said as he stood up and headed for the door.

"Oh, someone is whipped!" Pierce laughed.

"Better to be whipped than to need to go home and lie in bed alone. Come on, I'll drop you off at Ma's." Cade slapped his brother on his back and gave Cole a wink.

"I don't think you have any room to tease Cole when you live with your parents," Marshall teased as he scooped up what remained of Pierce's chips.

"Actually, I think I found a place."

"You did?" Marshall asked.

"Where?" Cade stopped at the door and looked at his little brother.

"You don't have any money to afford a place," Miles said, finally joining the conversation.

"I did. It's the abandoned Hunter property about three miles from here."

"I didn't know it was for sale or I'd have bought it. It joins part of my property," Miles contemplated. "It's around a hundred acres, isn't it?"

"Yup. And it's not for sale. But, I dug around the courthouse records and traced the owner through all the wills and approached them with an offer. They accepted and we sign the papers next week."

"Who's the owner?" Cade asked.

"Some woman in Ohio. She's the great-great-granddaughter of the original Hunter family. She's never been to the property and only inherited it three years ago when her father died. She's tired of paying the taxes on it, so she's willing to part with it at a good price."

"How are you affording to buy this place? You just graduated," Miles, the always business-oriented brother, asked.

"I've only been working since I was able to walk. When I was a teenager and finally started getting paid to work I started saving. Now I have enough for a sizable down payment and have already qualified for a Rural Development Loan."

"Congratulations little bro. Welcome to the ranks of us landowners. Do you know what you're going to do with the land?" Marshall asked as he put the cards away.

"I'm going to start clearing some of it for crops first. Then eventually I'll get around to tearing down the old house and building a new one."

"Our little brother is growing up," Cade teased. "Maybe next week we'll teach him how to shave." Cade ran a hand over his smooth chin and laughed when Pierce mimicked him, running his hand over his five o'clock shadow.

"I've been told it's sexy."

"Whatever you say lover boy. Come on, let's go." Cade grabbed him by the shoulder and gave him a shove.

"I'm coming too. Thanks for the game." Cole stood up and gave Marshall a pat on the back before heading out with Cade and Pierce.

Marshall grabbed a beer from the fridge and tossed it to Miles. He took a seat opposite him and stretched out his legs. Miles moved to sit on the edge of the couch and looked him right in the eye.

"I've been thinking about all these events recently. I think you need to be more careful. I know we've been out of the Army and back as civilians for a while now, but you need to tap those instincts and that training again. I'm pretty sure those shots were meant for you if you had been more visible."

"It's been killing me. I didn't even hear him. I know he was a couple hundred yards away, but it didn't even register to me when the woods went silent. It was all my fault. I won't make that mistake again." Marshall ran his hand over his face. The guilt had been eating away at him since that night.

"I know you've already looked into this, but I just did some research. I had no idea arms dealings, drug selling, and sex trading were all commonplace at big fights. I always thought they were some hicks who were just bored, but they're not. It's a big business if done right."

"I know. It amazed me too. I don't think we're at that level here though. Although I think our ring is making a play for the big leagues."

"Be smart and wear your vest at all times."

"Yes big brother," Marshall mocked. "Now that you're worried about me, tell me what's up with you."

"What do you mean?" Miles asked.

"You're acting different. Stressed, distant, and you're not even the one having dinner at the Wyatt's tomorrow. Something is going on that you don't like."

"It's nothing. Just a work issue."

Marshall looked at his brother and wanted to call it BS. But by the defensive body language Miles was displaying, he thought teasing may be better.

"Ah, the dangerous world of corporate agriculture."

"You have no idea. Just try to stay aware and safe. I need to get home. Call if you need me."

Miles left and Marshall took a sip of his beer. Miles had said to listen to his instincts and his instincts told him sooner or later, and whether Miles liked it or not, he was going to have to help his big brother out.

A knock at the door had him hoping Miles had changed his mind and had come back to ask for help. He opened the door and looked out at Ahmed.

"May I come in?"

"Oh, yeah, sure. You just missed poker night," Marshall said as he opened the door. Hopefully if Ahmed was here to kill him, he'd make it quick.

"I know. I waited outside for Miles to leave." Ahmed had his hands in his pocket and was looking around the house slowly.

"Oh." Dammit. He should have kept his firearm on him during poker. Pierce cheated anyway. At least he'd have a fighting chance against Ahmed.

"I wanted to talk to you about Katelyn."

"Yes?" Marshall asked when Ahmed didn't continue right away.

"We're good," he said as he brought his eyes to Marshall's.

"We are?"

"Yes."

"Are you sure?" Marshall asked.

"Yes. We're good. Goodnight." Ahmed held out his hand and Marshall shook it.

He smiled at Ahmed and walked him out the front door. He almost ran into Ahmed as he quickly stopped in his tracks.

"Your dog is in the tree."

"Oh, yeah, he likes the view up there," Marshall told him as he looked up at Bob sitting on a thick old tree limb.

The limb was thick and heavy. The end of it was just a couple feet off the ground. Bob liked to jump onto it and walk up it to where it leveled out about five feet above the ground.

"Have I mentioned your dog scares me? I swear he thinks he's smarter than us. I'm going to go before he starts talking to me."

"Ahmed," Marshall paused and waited for him to turn and look at him. "Thank you for coming over."

Ahmed just nodded and got into the car, never taking his eyes off Bob. Marshall waited for Ahmed to leave before turning to Bob.

"Really?"

Bob shook his ears and then slowly walked down the tree limb and strutted into the house, never looking back at him.

Marshall turned off his car and took ten deep breaths. When the Wyatts had insisted he come to dinner tonight, he had thought it was about them accepting him as part of Katelyn's life, but now he was unsure. For one thing there was Beauford standing by the door with a shotgun and a frown on his face.

Marshall pasted on a nervous smile and opened his door. He heard the crickets stop chirping as the gun cocked.

"You think you can make it through dinner with your clothes on, son?"

Marshall tried to fight the corners of his mouth from rising, but it was really hard when Mrs. Wyatt, dressed all in white, except for the scarlet red lipstick, swooped in and swatted Beauford on the arm with a handkerchief.

"Beauford, now that is no way to welcome our guests. Besides, I'm getting rather used to seeing him naked. The shock is quite gone I assure you. Now, come in dear."

He followed Mrs. Wyatt past Beauford and into a perfectly appointed formal dining room. A long table that could easily seat twenty was so well oiled it shined. Katelyn was setting the last plate down at the far end of the table.

A large crystal vase full of pink peonies sat in the center. Hand needlepointed placemats of the family crests with hundred-year-old bone china rimmed with real gold set on top of them. Displayed against one full wall were the horseshoes from all of Mrs. Wyatt's horses. Against the opposite wall were relics from her and Beauford's families' history ranging from the oil painting of some woman and child that looked to be from the 1700s, to a picture of Mr. and Mrs. Wyatt with Katelyn on graduation day at Auburn.

"Good evening Katelyn. You look beautiful. How are you feeling?" Marshall said in his most polite Southern gentleman voice.

She had on a long flowing light blue gauzy skirt with a tight white tank top that accented her body perfectly. "Hi. I'm feeling much better, thank you. I woke up this morning and was just a little sore, most of the pain was gone."

"Excellent. Is there anything I can do to help?"

"I was just about to bring out dinner. Why don't ya'll sit down?" Katelyn asked before disappearing through the swinging door into the kitchen. She was moving fast and he wondered if she was just as nervous as he was.

She was back before he had taken his seat and scooped out pecan-crusted chicken, green beans with chunks of bacon in them, and mashed potatoes. By the way she fidgeted all through dinner, he was sure his question had been answered. She was more nervous than he was. She had never sought her parents' approval so getting her grandparents' probably meant a lot to her.

He tried to sit straight and engage in the nicest of small talk. That should show her how serious he was about her. He did not do small talk. He was exhausted by the time the apple pie was eaten and tea was served and pretty sure he had done enough to please Mr. and Mrs. Wyatt.

"So, son, what are you doing to find the person who shot my granddaughter?" Shit. Beauford's eyes had narrowed again and there was no doubt that a gun was trained on him from under the table.

"I have a meeting with my deputies tomorrow to go over the suspects and interview the ones we find promising. I've been doing research all day and have it narrowed down to just a handful of people," he said confidently.

The Army and subsequent black ops he had gone on had taught him to never back down. It appeared that Beauford was not going to blink first. There was a rustling noise and then Beauford grunted and rubbed his leg under the table. Mrs. Wyatt turned to him and smiled wide.

"Sounds wonderful. I'm sure you're working very hard. How is Eugene, I mean Noodle, doing?" Mrs. Wyatt asked.

"Miss Lily is taking real good care of him. He's doing well enough that when Dr. Francis visits, he can get up and walk her to the door... under Miss Lily's supervision of course." He had never laughed harder than when Noodle called him the other night to see if he'd arrest Miss Lily for assault with a broom.

"Well, it's getting late," Katelyn said as she rose from her seat. "I'll walk him out."

Marshall stood, said his goodnights, and thanked the Wyatts for dinner. Katelyn had been so quiet through dinner that he had desperately wanted to sit next to her, hold her hand, and reassure her that he wasn't going anywhere. As soon as they reached the front of the house he felt her tension slip away as she reached for him, laying her hand on his arm.

"Wow. That was worse than any press interview I've ever given." Yup, she'd been nervous alright. Dinner had been nothing compared to some of his interrogations he'd both given and received.

"It wasn't bad, Katelyn. I love your family."

She smiled and he knew the timing was right. One kiss and then he'd tell her how much he loved her. He brushed a strand of her long hair away from her face and slid his arm around her waist, pulling her against him before lowering his lips to hers.

Her body melted into his as he tightened his grip and deepened the kiss. This was it. It was the perfect moment. He broke the kiss and pulled back just far enough to look into her eyes.

"Katelyn, I have wanted to tell you something for so long now."

"And I've wanted to kiss you like this all night."

She leaned forward and his words were lost on her tongue. His words of love were lost in the heat of the moment and he slid his hand down and cupped her round bottom. The moment was magic. The kiss, the hands, the sound of a gun being cocked.

"Goodnight, son."

He moved his hand off of Katelyn's bottom and gave her bright-red face a quick peck before turning toward Beauford.

"Goodnight." He gave Beauford an innocent smile and then squeezed Katelyn's hand.

"Beauford, get in here or he'll never propose," Mrs. Wyatt hissed from the door.

"Oh Sweet Pea, I'll make sure he does. Don't you worry your pretty little head about that."

Propose? Shoot, he couldn't even tell Katelyn he loved her. When could he ever propose? Not that he was thinking about that, or was he?

Marshall took a gulp of his drink and then took another bite of the bread pudding Miss Daisy had just put down in front of him. He needed a snack before everyone met at his house to go over all the data they had put together.

"I heard you had a visitor last night," Miss Violet said as she topped off his drink.

"I did?"

"That's right. Jasmine was in here last night talking about how she was heading over to your place to spend the night. So, whose bed did your boots sleep under last night, or should I say, whose boots were under your bed?" Marshall would have been shocked if he hadn't known the Rose sisters his whole life.

"They were under my bed, all night long."

"And were you in that bed all by your lonesome?"

"No. Someone all warm and soft kept stealing my pillow."

"I knew it! That Jasmine is one sneaky and determined woman. Did I win the bet Daisy Mae?"

"Wait, are you telling me there's a bet about Bob stealing my pillow at night?"

"Bob? I thought...Oh you rascal!" She swatted him with a dishrag and tried to glare at him, but she was laughing too hard.

"I don't know Miss Violet, I'm really hurt. I can't believe you would think I'd sleep with Jasmine. You really think she's my type?"

"Goodness no. I think Katelyn's your type, but nothing is really progressing there and when Jasmine was in here bragging about you and her, I thought maybe she was the reason things were stalled with you and Katelyn."

"I have no idea what Jasmine's talking about but I won't forget you didn't have faith in me. Nope. You're going to have to make some of that delicious chocolate torte to make me forgive you." He gave her a wink as he placed some cash on the table and headed out for his meeting.

Katelyn pulled into the back of the house and parked her car. She had to go back to the clinic to check on some of her patients. It was late and she just wanted to get to bed. She walked in through the sunroom off the kitchen and found her grandma feeding slices of steak to Alice.

"Hi Nana." Katelyn looked around for Ruffles. Lately she and Alice had been attached at the hip. "Where's Ruffles?"

"She went out a while ago, but I don't think she's come back. I'll ask your grandfather."

Katelyn gave Alice a good neck scratch as she waited for her grandmother to return. Ruffles was probably just curled up in her grandfather's office.

"Sorry dear, he hasn't seen her for about an hour. She probably went into the pasture to roll in horse poo. You know how she loves to do that."

"Ugh. She does, and my old designer just sent her that really great collar! I better go find her before she ruins it."

Katelyn got up slowly and had a desire to stomp her foot. She was tired and the last thing she wanted to do was stomp through the pasture avoiding horse poop and dragging her stinky dog home. Then there was bathing and drying her hair. It would be past midnight at this point before she could go to bed.

"Take a flashlight Katelyn! It's pitch black out there. And don't go too far. Do you want me to call Joey and have him go with you?" her grandmother asked as she handed her a flashlight from the drawer.

"No thanks. I don't want to bother him when he has to get up so early in the morning. I'll be back in a couple of minutes. I'm sure she's in that pasture behind the mare's barn with all the fresh poop."

Katelyn tried to laugh at the idea of this prissy white poodle with a shiny new pink Tiffany's dog collar rolling in cow poop, but drudging through pastures this late at night knowing she was going to have to bathe said poodle wasn't too funny. She stomped down the path with the light from the flashlight bouncing as she went around the house and past the mare barn into the darkness of the night.

Chapter Seventeen

Marshall poured another cup of coffee for Dinky, refilled Annie's glass of water and tossed some treats to where Bob sat in one of the chairs before sitting down at his dining room table. The dark cherry wood was hidden under stacks of criminal reports, highlighted maps, and enlarged copies of driver's licenses. They had been working for most of the night. They pulled the records on everyone with a criminal history and worked their way down to a few suspects.

"I think these six people look promising," Marshall said as he sat back down at the table. "Although we're just looking at a snippet of information. Now that we have some suspects based on location and local criminal history, let's run a national search on them and their families to see what we get."

"I'll run it now." Annie pulled her laptop over to her and started typing in the names one at a time and waited for the information to pop up on the screen.

"I don't know, Dink, I have a feeling about these two." Marshall tapped the pictures of Andre and Camille Watkins. "Annie, can you run them next?"

"Sure. I just got the reports back on the Simpson brothers and nothing out of the ordinary for them. They're focused more on petty crimes than anything to do with animals, guns, or drugs."

"What about this guy? He had his house condemned twice by the health department and both times they found pit bulls caged in the basement," Dinky said as he tapped a file.

"True, although they were neglected. They were skin and bones and not even close to aggressive, but we'll have Annie check him out next."

Marshall looked over the map again and focused on the areas not marked. It just seemed like too much of a coincidence that the Watkins' house was right at the mid-point of the crimes. When he placed the crimes on a map, they formed an arch and the Watkins' house was just around five miles from all the sites.

"I think we got something here," Annie said as she scanned the screen of her laptop.

"What've you got?" Marshall asked as he stood up to look over Annie's shoulder.

"It seems that the Watkins have a criminal history far more than what we thought. In Georgia they were arrested for animal cruelty. They had too many dogs within the Atlanta city limits and they were housed in poor conditions. When animal patrol investigated they found the dogs had been abused. There was evidence of dog fighting, but not enough to convict on that count. The dogs were all pit bulls and were taken away from them.

"The Watkins' both served three weeks in jail for abuse and as soon as they were released they moved to Lipston, Kentucky where Andre Watkins had a brother. His brother, Jerry Watkins, was arrested a short time later for felony assault and battery and illegal possession of firearms. Now, this is where it gets interesting. Jerry still owns a tract of land here in Kentucky — a tract of land that just happens to connect to the county property near the house that blew up."

"I think that's enough for a warrant, don't you?" Marshall smiled. "Dinky, call Sheriff Nuggett and fill him in, then wake up Judge Cooper and get us a warrant. Make sure you have Nuggett call as soon as a warrant comes through so we can work on this together.

Annie, email everything you have to Nuggett now so he can forward it on to a judge in case we cross the county line. Then email it to Judge Cooper."

Marshall glanced at his watch—it was almost eleven. It was going to take most of the night to get everything prepared. He better get his equipment together, grab a bite to eat, and then try to get a couple hours sleep before Nuggett called.

"Nuggett said he'll call you as soon as the warrant comes in. Judge Cooper said he'd start to look everything over in a couple minutes. What do you want us to do now?" Dinky asked as he hung up the phone.

"Annie, I want you to go home for the night. You'll handle press coverage if there is any tomorrow."

"I'm guessing this is for my own good so I'll dutifully do it. Although, I'll be really mad if I miss a shootout. You know how I love shooting bad guys," Annie mumbled as she gathered her things.

"I know. If there's shooting involved, I'll let you do the interrogations so you don't miss all the fun," Marshall joked. Annie was a lot of fun and one damn good deputy.

"Deal! You boys don't have too much fun without me," Annie gave a little wave to the guys, a kiss to Bob, and headed to her car.

"I'll go to the station and check our supplies to get ready for the call."

"Thanks, Dinky."

Marshall rolled his shoulders to stretch and then started to clean up the dining room table. It was time to get something to eat and then check his supplies for the raid.

He stopped stacking papers when he heard a noise come from the kitchen. Dammit, if Bob was opening drawers again he was going to lose it. The other night he had come downstairs at two in the morning, after waking from another nightmare, to find Bob on his hind legs with the top drawer open and munching on a bag of chips.

"Bob! I swear, if you're getting into my drawers again it's dry dog food for a week for you!"

Marshall put down the papers and listened. The noise had stopped but Bob wasn't coming into the dining room pretending like he hadn't done anything wrong either.

Marshall's instincts flared to life. It wasn't Bob in the kitchen. He piled up the dishes and sauntered into the kitchen as if nothing was wrong. An island stood before him and if he was right, the person in his house was behind it. He set the dishes on the island and then picked up one dish and dropped it. The dish shattered on the tan tiled floor.

"Damn," Marshall said as he knelt down to pick up the pieces.

He picked up the largest sliver of china and palmed it as he pretended to pick up the broken pieces. He felt the air shift and knew it was time to make his move. He sprung forward and catapulted himself over his island. His hands were stretched outright to grab the guy and take him down. He felt his legs drag across the marble countertops as he plowed into the chest of the black-clad form that had risen from his hiding place.

With a whoosh of air the man fell to the ground. Marshall landed on top of him and, with a quick movement of his arm, sliced the man in black across the forearm as they struggled for power. Marshall blocked a punch and landed a solid one of his own in the man's stomach. Marshall felt the knee to his kidney and rolled away from the attack. He leapt to his feet at the same time the man in black did.

Marshall took in the black shirt, pants, and the face covered with a ski mask. He only had a second before the man charged him. He tossed the sharp shard of china into his left hand and waited. Timing was everything after all. Marshall held his ground as the man charged. At the last second he took a small step to the left. The man's momentum carried him past Marshall and he gave the man a good shove in the back. The man ran into the small kitchen table and fell to the ground with a groan.

Marshall wasted no time. He reached down and grabbed the man by the back of the neck and hauled him upright, slamming his face into the wall. He struggled and thrashed as Marshall tried to pin his arms. Marshall finally managed to grab a wrist and wrench it behind the man's back.

"What are you doing here?" Marshall growled.

"Go to hell!" the man spat.

Marshall pulled up on the man's arm harder until he shouted out in pain.

"I'll ask you one more time. Next time, the shoulder comes out. What are you doing here?"

Marshall heard the slight clicking of Bob's nails on the tile and watched out of the corner of his eyes as Bob casually strode in. Bob yawned and took a look around the kitchen before walking over to the upturned kitchen table. He jumped into one of the chairs that was still standing and stared at the man pinned to the wall.

"What's your dog doing, man? He's really freaking me out."

Marshall hid his smile behind the man's back. Bob just sat there staring the man in his eyes with a little drool hanging from his mouth. When he licked his lips Marshall narrowed his eyes as he saw that Bob's normally pink tongue was brown with melting chocolate. How on earth had he opened the cabinet upstairs where he hid his secret candy stash?

"He's just waiting for me to give the command and then he'll rip your throat out. See how he's licking his lips in anticipation." Marshall bit his lip so as to not laugh. Bob had a bored look on his face and had never attacked anything, unless you counted chocolate and pizza.

"Call him off and I'll tell you everything." The man was starting to get nervous.

"Tell me and then I'll call him off."

"Fine. I was hired to be a distraction. I was supposed to beat you up enough for you to have to go to the hospital."

"A distraction from what? Who hired you?"

"There's a big dog fight tonight. A guy named Andre hired me a couple days ago. Now, call off that dog."

"Where's the fight?"

"I don't know man. I told you everything I know," he whined.

"Come on, you're coming with me."

He pulled the man's arm and led him away from Bob toward the cruiser as he read him his rights. He shoved him into the back of the car and ran inside. He strapped on his flak vest, threw on his shoulder holsters, and strapped a large knife and gun to his thigh.

It was happening now. Somewhere the fight had started and all the players were there. He picked up his radio and called Dinky as he started the car. He needed to pick up Katelyn in case of injury to the dogs. Then he needed to patrol all the woods in Keeneston as fast as he could. He pulled out his cell phone and dialed Katelyn's number. He waited impatiently as it rang and then went to voicemail.

Katelyn walked down the path behind the yearling barn and froze. Her imagination was playing tricks on her. She was seeing things in the shadows and hearing things on the wind.

"Ruffles?" She spoke quietly as she came to the end of the building.

Katelyn was jumpy. Her heart was pounding, the hair was standing up on her arms, and she had started to breathe heavily. She told herself she was just being silly. She pressed herself against the black painted wood and made herself calm down. She listened in the night air, but all was quiet.

"I'm such a silly goose," she said to herself as she pushed off the rough wooden wall of the barn and rounded the corner.

A movement in the shadow of the barn caught her attention a second before a hand covered her mouth. She screamed, but the hand held it back. From the darkness of the shadow, a second figure emerged slowly. The only thing she could see was the glowing white of his teeth as he smiled and the barbwire tattoo across his pale neck.

She gulped for breath as panic overtook her. She felt her nostrils flare as she tried to get oxygen to her brain. Her breaths were coming shorter and things were starting to blur. The man came closer until he was just feet in front of her. She fought with all she had, but the hand over her mouth and across her chest just squeezed tighter.

"Nice to see you again Dr. Jacks," the man said with a twang from the Deep South.

She paused for a moment in her struggles and looked at the man. He smiled at her then. Slowly. She blinked and before she could compute what was happening his fist slammed into her face and everything went black.

Chapter Eighteen

Katelyn's head swam as noises assaulted her. Cheers, barking, and screeching reached her before she could open her eyes. She then smelled the blood thick in the air, the pot smoke dancing under her nose, and she felt heavy pressure gripping her wrists.

Her eyes fluttered back and she instinctually tried to jump backward. She was near a wooden ring. A snarling pit bull had another dog by the neck. The dog was screaming in pain. Fear that Katelyn had never known before slammed her in the gut as she involuntarily threw up. She tried to wipe her mouth only to find two very large men were holding her hands tightly.

"Ah, good, you're awake. The next fight is in your honor. Just look right over there where my beautiful wife is standing," the man with the barbwire tattoo said to her.

She scanned to where he pointed and screamed like she had never screamed before.

"Ruffles! Let her go! Ruffles, no no no!"

Katelyn fought with every ounce of strength she had. She begged and pleaded for someone to help her, but instead of helping they all laughed and pointed. Tears rolled down her face as she fought to get to her best friend. Ruffles was barking and trying to break free, when Katelyn saw the woman slam her hand down on her snout. Ruffles cried out in pain and the woman laughed.

"Please, I'll do anything, just let her go."

"We will, we'll let her go when she gets in the ring next. I'm sorry to say the odds are against her. But if she makes it out, we'll let her go. Now, you're another story."

Marshall had a bad feeling as he drove up to the Wyatt Estate and saw the back of Katelyn's car sticking out from behind the house. Dinky was starting a search with Keeneston and Lipston deputies. He was going to join them as soon as he picked up Katelyn.

Marshall parked the car at the front door and hurried up the stairs to ring the doorbell. The place was quiet and mostly dark, but nothing seemed wrong. However, he just couldn't shake the feeling that something bad was happening.

The light over the door flipped on and Beauford opened the door with Mrs. Wyatt right behind him. Beauford was still dressed in a black three-piece suit, but Mrs. Wyatt had on her dressing gown and bright red lipstick as if she had just applied it.

"Sheriff, what can we do for you this late at night?" Beauford asked, clearly agitated.

"I'm trying to reach Katelyn, but she's not answering her phone."

"She's not answering for us either. She went out a little while ago looking for Ruffles and hasn't come back yet. We were actually going to call you. It's not like her to be gone for so long." Mrs. Wyatt wrung her wrinkled hands together and the foreboding feeling he had felt just moments ago took its place in his chest, smothering him.

"Which direction did she go?"

"That way, past the mare's barn," Mrs. Wyatt said as she pointed.

Marshall didn't wait, he bolted down the stairs and took off at a dead run toward the barn. He didn't even realize it, but he had already pulled his gun as he approached the barn. The second he had heard Katelyn was missing his mind and body had switched instantly to combat mode.

As he passed the mares and approached the yearling barn, he heard the sound of the young colts and fillies crunching on their feed and shifting slightly in their stalls. Cautiously, but efficiently, he scanned the area and determined it was clear. A light at the end of the barn drew his attention as he ran the length of the barn.

He stopped just short of the end of the barn and let his senses search the night. Crickets chirped and owls hooted. There were no dark shadows moving around and he knew it was clear. He rounded the barn and found the source of the light. A flashlight lay on the ground, its beam casting a warm glow into the nearby pasture.

He didn't have to think twice, he knew it was Katelyn's. He scanned the area and took in the pasture to his left, the barn behind him, another pasture, and barn in the distance on the right. In front of him lay a narrow paved road that ran between the pastures and into the darkness. He knew when he and Katelyn surveyed the area that it led to the back of the property and was the most likely direction they took her.

Marshall ran down the lane. Years of military training had him pacing himself into a fast run because he knew it would be a couple of miles to the back of the property. He didn't want to risk taking the car, knowing the people who took her would be on the lookout for headlights or listening for the noise of an engine.

It took him just twelve minutes to cover the two plus miles to the back of the farm. He slowed then and made sure to slow his breathing. The woods sat in front of him and they could be anywhere in them. He thought back to the map of the area and the location of the fights. He was close to where Mrs. Wyatt had found them, and knew they wouldn't be stupid enough to go back to the same place. The map also showed an area some three miles down and across the county line where Nuggett had found evidence of training. That was enough to go on. They'd be somewhere around a mile or mile and a half into the woods. Marshall jogged into the darkness of the woods and disappeared into the shadows of the night.

Katelyn pulled so hard against the men holding her she thought her shoulders had come out of joint. Her wrists burned as she struggled to free herself, pulling again and again against the tight grip of the men.

The woman had pulled Ruffles over to the ring. Ruffles' nose flared at the smell of the blood and her eyes widened in fear as she saw the large, snarling brindle pit bull in the ring being held by a large, muscled man. Ruffles started to pant heavily and leaped backwards, choking on the tight collar.

Katelyn screamed until she felt blood trickle down her throat and her voice stopped coming. She thrashed and kicked at the men holding her as sobs racked her body. The woman opened the gate to the ring as Ruffles jerked violently against the leash. Katelyn's heart stopped when the woman dragged Ruffles into the ring and slipped off the leash.

"I'm afraid it won't be a good fight, but it'll be entertaining nonetheless," Andre said as he came to stand by her.

"There's a special place in Hell waiting for you," she managed to choke out.

Her eyes never left Ruffles as she watched her scratch at the door of the ring looking for escape.

Marshall heard the cheers and saw the portable lights a mile into the woods. He slowed his approach and stayed in the shadows. He knew there would be sentries keeping a lookout for law enforcement. He moved slowly and kept away from the lights. He moved along the perimeter and located the two lookouts. He was pretty sure he could get past them both without being seen.

He was evaluating the best entrance when he saw Katelyn. She was being held between two men. They each had her by the wrist as she struggled, but what was worse was they each had a gun in their other hand. She was sobbing and struggling with all she had. He followed where she was looking and saw the white poof of Ruffles' head popping up from the ring as she tried to leap over the five-foot wall. With a surge of effort, he saw Katelyn try to pull free again only to have one of the men raise a gun and press it against her head.

Blind anger overtook him and sneaking in to rescue Katelyn was no longer an option. He moved the gun he was holding into his left hand and pulled out the Glock from his shoulder holster with his right. He aimed and fired with no hesitation. The man with the gun froze and then dropped to the ground. Katelyn tried to scream again as the other man holding her brought her against him. He used her as a shield and fired off a shot in Marshall's direction.

Marshall held his ground and in a split second fired off another shot hitting the man in the shoulder. He fell to the ground as gunfire erupted all around him. He saw Katelyn shake her fallen captor off and run toward the ring.

Marshall dove for cover behind a tree and fired at a man who had pulled out a .45 and had started to shoot in Marshall's direction. He heard the yelling and screaming of people who had just realized a serious gunfight was underway instead of just weapon testing. Someone had shouted that the cops were here and people started to scatter. However, some wanted in on the action and had pulled various weapons out.

"Ruffles!" Katelyn's shriek rose above the other noise and he looked around the tree to see her pulling herself over the wall of the ring. There was a large man with a dog in the ring that looked thrilled to have a new play toy. He advanced on her and Ruffles.

"Shit!"

Marshall ducked low and started running for the ring. It couldn't be that easy though, he had to get through eight people by his quick count. Just another day in the office, he thought as he hurdled over a table and plowed into a man with a beer gut the size of a keg and a sawed-off shotgun at his side. He had to make it to Katelyn. Nothing and no one else mattered.

Katelyn felt the moment her wrist was released and tried to pull away from her one remaining captor. Before she had the chance she was hauled up and spun around. The first thing she noticed was the man on the ground with a bullet wound in his head. Who did that?

She looked into the woods and saw a huge hulking shadow with two guns raised looking like a sinister devil emerging from the dark.

She didn't know who it was, but at that moment she didn't care. The man who held her moved her so she was in between him and the devil. Before she even had a chance to worry, a second shot was fired off and the man holding her was hurled backward, his gun dropping to the ground as he fell.

She sure as hell wasn't going to wait around to find out who was shooting at them. Katelyn shook off the man's sweaty grip on her now raw wrist and sprinted for the ring. Her hands bit into the jagged wood at the top of the wall as she pulled herself up. Her feet slid as she tried to climb the smooth side of the wall until she fell forward and into the dirt ring.

Ruffles yipped and bounded over to her. She flung her arms around her dog's soft furry neck and cried as she felt Ruffles shaking in fear. But, then she heard it. The noise sent chills up her back and she froze with her arms around Ruffles. Turning her head to the low laughter she saw the man with a black leather vest smiling at her with his muscles bulging. He still held the huge brindle pit bull.

"Two for one, Sampson," his low voice rumbled with glee as he leaned down and unhooked the leash.

Katelyn scrambled backward as the sound of growls and gunfire reached her. She stood to her full height and shoved Ruffles behind her. No one was going to get her dog.

Marshall didn't have time to reload. He tossed the gun on the ground and grabbed the spare Glock from his leg holster. People were shooting and not really knowing who to shoot at. Others were running around grabbing their things and trying to run through the woods to hide or to escape. Dogs barked, guns were fired, people were screaming, but he never lost sight of Katelyn.

He fired a shot at a drugged-out shirtless man with a ponytail, who was randomly firing a gun at anything that moved and pushed past two women huddled together in miniskirts and not much else.

He kept his calm and remembered to breathe. With a cold and meticulous calculation, he dispensed with any obstacle in his way. He had seen the man advance on Katelyn and soon he was near enough to scale the wall when he was hit over the head with a bottle.

Marshall felt the bottle crack over his skull and for a second his vision went blurry. In that moment rage overtook him as he whirled around and with a quick kick took out the knee of the drunken man with tattoos covering most of his visible body. He went down with a howl and Marshall silenced him with a right cross.

He turned back to the wall and vaulted over it and into the ring. The man with the leather vest just smiled and pulled out a large blade. He didn't have time to look at Katelyn as he aimed his gun and fired. Nothing. He was out. He waited until the man was closer and then threw the gun as hard as he could, hitting the man in the face. It didn't do any damage, but it did give him time to formulate a brief plan of attack. He pulled out his knife as the man swiped away the blood running down the side of his face.

Katelyn looked at the man and the dog, guessing the dog was more dangerous. She pulled herself up and in her sternest voice yelled at the dog. Unfortunately, he was too much like his owner and just found it amusing as he stalked her and Ruffles.

Suddenly the devil figure bounded over the wall and landed in the ring with a gun drawn. She couldn't believe it. It was Marshall. He was here! Hope soared in her until she heard the click of his gun. Empty. He was going to be killed! She watched in horror as he pulled out a knife and held it so it lay against his forearm. He and the man started to circle each other lashing out with their knives in battle. The man slashed and then threw a vicious hook. Marshall was able to block the knife, but the man's fist crashed into his eye.

The dog took advantage of her distraction and lunged. It was too late to react, she had lost focus. She waited for the pain of the massive jaws to clamp down on her arm and she closed her eyes in fear. Instead of feeling the pain of the vise-like grip she heard the most horrific war cry. Her eyes flew open just in time to see Ruffles meeting the dog in a mid-air collision, the force of the hundred pound pit bull knocking her to the ground with a loud thud.

The dog landed on top of her, his mouth open and ready for the kill as Katelyn screamed and lunged forward. A menacing growl came from behind her and Katelyn braced for another attack from a loose dog. A black dog streaked through the air and over the wall, landing on top of the big brindle and sinking its teeth into his thick skin. The dog was much too small and was easily tossed by the brindle. The black dog with the pink collar landed near Katelyn and she gasped — Alice!

Katelyn dove for Ruffles and put herself in front of her to protect her from the brindle that was advancing on them. She wanted to scream for Marshall, but one look showed that he was fighting for his life. The sound of metal against metal rang out in the ring.

The dog lunged again and Alice threw herself in front of Ruffles and Katelyn, growling and snapping at the brindle that was easily twice her size. Katelyn chanced a glance at Marshall and stopped breathing when she saw the man thrust at him, his knife hitting Marshall right in the stomach. Marshall bent over slightly, but hooked his knife into the man's side before falling back.

"No!" she screamed. Tears streamed down her cheeks and she felt as if her heart had been pierced with the knife as well.

She watched as he fell, rolled, and then grabbed the brindle's discarded leash before bounding up. A large cut was in his t-shirt revealing the flak vest underneath. She breathed a sigh of relief but it was cut short as the brindle dog lunged at Alice again. Marshall snapped the leather leash as he raced toward the dog. The loud noise drew his attention away from Alice and solely onto Marshall. The two circled each other as Marshall widened the loop at the end of the slip lead.

The dog lunged and Marshall slid the leash over his head and pulled tight. They struggled, dog thrashing, man holding on for power until Marshall was able to maneuver the dog to one of the hooks in the wall and tie him up. The dog jumped and snarled, but couldn't get free.

"Come on, let's get out of here."

"Ruffles was knocked down hard. It looks like she has a bite on her shoulder too. She saved my life," she cried, petting Ruffles' head as she lay on the bloody dirt floor.

"Get the door, I got her. What a good girl you are, Alice. I don't know how you got here, but thank God you did."

Alice thumped her tail and gave him a kiss when he bent to pick up Ruffles. He carried her out of the ring and looked over the clearing. People lay injured or dead in the trampled grass, either from his doing or their own. When the gunshots started some people realized he was a cop and started shooting at him, but others just started shooting. Soon it was hard to tell who was shooting whom in the crossfire. Tables and chairs were knocked over. Some people were still trying to get their stuff together while others had sped away in their cars.

"We've gotta get out of here. Go that way, through the woods," Marshall nodded his head across the clearing.

Katelyn led the way for him with Alice sticking close to Ruffles as he carried her through the clearing. Ruffles barked in pain whenever her shoulder was moved. Katelyn was anxious to get to safety and look her over. If they could get into the woods, he wouldn't feel so exposed. They were approaching the tree line when he heard Alice start to growl.

"Katelyn, wait," he loudly whispered.

"Yes, why don't you wait? Didn't your mother ever teach you not to go playing in the woods at night? It's not safe." Andre stepped out of the darkness with a gun held level to her head.

Marshall's hand tightened on the knife he still held, hidden under Ruffles. He wished he had kept a hold of all his guns. After he ran through his magazines, he had just tossed the guns where he was at that time. So, they lay in various places in the clearing and one in the fighting ring.

"Yes, the big bad wolf may get you," a woman laughed as she came out from a different part of the woods holding a rifle aimed at Marshall.

Marshall recognized them instantly. It was Andre and Camille Watkins. The large barbwire tattoo on his neck was a dead giveaway.

"You have messed everything up for us again. We had top leaders from all the important divisions in the international level and you embarrassed us. You think I'm going to just let you walk away after you ruined our lives?"

Andre stalked forward and shoved Marshall to the ground. Alice growled and ran to Ruffles as she fell to the ground. Katelyn had made a move towards him, but Camille stopped her by shoving the barrel of her rifle into her side. Andre loomed over Marshall, his large Smith and Wesson .44 Magnum revolver held loosely in his hand as he pointed it at Marshall's head.

"What exactly did we ruin?" Marshall asked, needing time to change his position so he had a chance at knocking the gun out of Andre's hand.

"We had drug and weapons dealers from all over the world here tonight. We had representatives from the International Warrior's Association. We were this close to being invited to join and get out of this Podunk town! And you ruined it, just like you did last time. I should've killed you and her when I had the chance instead of just playing with you."

"The guy who came to pay me a visit seemed to want to do more than just play."

"A lot of good that did. He'll be next on my list after I get done with you."

Andre pulled the hammer back on the gun, the sound of it clicking into place reverberated through the clearing. Marshall shoved himself forward and landed a square hit on Andre's knees, sending him teetering backward, and landing hard on his backside.

Marshall scrambled for the gun in Andre's hand while Andre clawed at him with his free hand, trying to fight him off. They rolled on the grass—Andre trying to aim the gun and Marshall managing to hold him off as his fingers climbed up Andre's arm toward the gun.

With a swift motion, Marshall brought his knee up and repeatedly struck Andre in the kidney as he used his arms to hold him in place. Andre grunted and brought the gun down on his shoulder. Marshall used both hands to grab at the large gun. He shot out his elbow and heard the satisfying crunch of Andre's nose. Andre instinctively reached for his nose and Marshall took full advantage. He wretched the gun away from Andre and with a strong punch to the midsection sent him rolling on the ground in pain.

"Not so fast. You move and I kill her," Camille said from behind Katelyn. Marshall looked for a clear shot, but couldn't see one.

"Now, I'd be much obliged if you put that gun down and let go of my granddaughter." Beauford's stern southern voice rung clear through the woods.

Camille whipped around and hesitated at the sight of Beauford in a three-piece suit holding an antique rifle almost as big as her.

"Bless your heart, you better do what he says, because if he doesn't shoot you, I certainly will." Mrs. Wyatt emerged from the woods holding her own vintage Remington rifle steadily in her hands. Her white dressing gown blew gently in the night air and her red lips stretched into a thin line as she cocked her gun.

Camille dropped her gun and held up her hands all while cursing and saying some very nasty things about Katelyn. Beauford moved to stand over Andre as Marshall rushed to Katelyn. He wrapped her in his arms and kissed her as though both of theirs lives depended on it.

She was still shaking as he put his lips to hers. He pulled her close, running his hands through her long tangled hair. She was alive. He forgot about everything but her. He forgot until the sound of two gunshots rang out. Marshall jumped back with Andre's gun raised as he scanned the woods.

"You fucking shot me!" Camille screamed at Mrs. Wyatt.

"Oh Lord, the bastard shot me. I'm dying. I know I am," Andre cried as he cradled his foot.

"Oh hush, it was just a nick," Beauford calmly said.

"What the hell just happened?" Marshall demanded.

"Well, you know, I'm old and this gun is just oh so heavy," Mrs. Wyatt drawled. "It just slipped. See, I thought she was going for her gun and tried to aim mine in self-defense, but it was just too heavy for an old woman like myself." She shrugged her shoulders, not looking the least bit feeble.

"You shot me because I said I should've gutted that useless cotton ball of a dog and that worthless mutt in the pink collar. I remember her. She was the worst dog I've ever seen," Camille spit out.

"No wonder you shot her. Good job Nana," Katelyn said as she put her arm around her grandmother and stared daggers at Camille who lay clutching her side. "Nice aim there, Nana."

"I thought you'd appreciate the irony of that," Mrs. Wyatt said as she made sure to be careful of her granddaughter's wound on her side.

"Beauford?" Marshall asked as he pinched his nose.

"The SOB tried to kill my granddaughter and my dog. He deserves a lot more than what I gave him."

"I'm sure it was in self-defense though, right?"

"No. Oh! Oh, yes Sheriff. I thought he had a weapon and I was defending my family."

"He sure did. I thought I was going to have to shoot them myself," Annie said as she and Dinky walked into the clearing.

"Me too. What do you want us to do now Sheriff?" Dinky asked as he looked around.

"Annie, call in medical and call Nuggett. He'll want to be here for this. How did you all know where we were?"

"Mrs. Wyatt called dispatch and said that Alice had run off and they were following her. They told us the direction and we followed the tire marks and holes in the fences," Dinky explained.

"And you Annie?" Marshall asked impatiently.

"I promised I'd wait in the car if I heard any gunfire." Annie said as if she were a teenager trying to get out of trouble for breaking curfew.

Marshall shrugged, that was as good as he was going to get. Although, he hadn't seen any holes in the fences when he was running here. He must have been so focused he didn't see them.

"Dinky, cuff them and read them their rights." Marshall handed over Andre's gun to Annie and pulled Katelyn to him. "There's been something I have wanted to tell you for the longest time."

Chapter Nineteen

Marshall took Katelyn by the hands and stepped away from the crowd as Annie and Dinky transported the Watkinses to the patrol cars and set up a perimeter around the area.

"Katelyn, I know you want to get to Ruffles, but I have to tell you something," Marshall said gently as he looked into her eyes.

"Yes?" she asked uncertainly.

"I..."

"Marshall! Katelyn! Oh thank God you're okay," Miss Lily cried as she and her sisters got out of her Buick and hurried to the crime scene tape.

"Son of..." Marshall growled.

"What were you going to say?" Katelyn asked.

"Never mind. We'll talk soon, okay?"

"Okay. I better get to Ruffles before Alice licks her to death."

"Ladies. How did you know where we were?"

"Edith was filling in on dispatch," Miss Lily said with a shrug as if that explained everything, which it did. Edith was only second to John Wolfe in spreading gossip.

"Ah, yes, I forgot tonight was her night. So, I should expect the rest of the town shortly," Marshall said sarcastically.

"I'd give it ten minutes. Ruth! Ruth, dear, are you alright?"

Ruth and Beauford made their way over to the police tape to fill their friends in on the action. Katelyn was setting Ruffles' shoulder.

Annie was taking pictures. Dinky had started to get names of the wounded and was reading them their rights. Many of them had their weapons nearby and drugs still on them. The jail would be full tonight.

"You shot her!" Miss Violet gasped at Mrs. Wyatt.

"Accidently! She accidently shot them in self-defense. That was their official statement to me and we're sticking with that." Marshall felt a very big headache coming on.

"Well of course it was accidently. Accidently on purpose. Good for you Ruth. But, make sure when Kenna gets here you look pale and weak. She hasn't been here long enough to remember you were an alternate on the Olympic Rifle team," Miss Daisy said as all the Rose sisters nodded.

Oh God, Marshall was sure he was going to jail, but there was no way he'd send Mrs. Wyatt there. Sheriff Nugget, Kenna and Will pulled up at the same time. Before they made it over to the crime scene, Henry pulled up in his new Lexus and got out in one of his shiny suits. It was almost one in the morning, why he was in a suit was beyond anyone's imagination. Kenna had obviously been asleep. Her hair was sticking out in different directions and her shoes didn't match.

"Sheriff, we got them. Kenna, you'll have no problem prosecuting them, although most of them will be heading up to federal court I think," Marshall told them.

"I guessed that and put in a call to the U.S. Assistant Attorney. She'll be calling you in the morning to set up a meeting. After their trial, we'll prosecute on smaller charges if we feel like they need more time in jail."

"So, what happened to them? Did they get shot in the crossfire?" Sheriff Nuggett asked as he nodded to the Watkinses being loaded onto stretchers.

"Um, no. Mr. and Mrs. Wyatt shot them in self-defense when they thought they were reaching for a weapon."

"Who, them?" Nuggett asked looking over to where Mr. and Mrs. Wyatt were standing. "Christ, they don't look they could even lift a gun. No wonder their aims were so far off."

Marshall choked as he glanced over his shoulder at the Wyatts. Beauford was hunched over and using his rifle as a cane. Mrs. Wyatt was in the middle of what could only be called the vapors. Marshall turned to where a truck with a flashing light was approaching, followed by a large box van painted black.

"I called Cole to assist since we have a lot of people to process and a lot of the charges will be federal. I also called the DEA to help with all the drugs around," Annie said as she approached the group.

"Blake! How the hell are you?" Special Agent in Charge Vincent Romero said as he stepped down from the box truck.

"Good, thank you. But, it's Davies now," Annie said as she shook her former boss's hand.

"That's right. Left us at the DEA for the football coach, how's he doing?"

"He's good. We're going to have a baby around Christmas," Annie told him.

"Then what the hell are you doing out here? Go home at once!"

"I tried that already. It didn't work," Marshall sighed. "She doesn't take orders very well."

"True. So, what's going on Sheriff?"

Marshall took Romero around to introduce him to all the people working the scene as he filled him in on the dog-fighting ring and all the subsequent drugs and weapons that were found.

Marshall had never filled out so much paperwork in his life. He interviewed everyone who was able to talk and only got more frustrated. Although they had gotten the Watkinses, they were still missing two crucial players. He had learned from the interviews that there was a beautiful woman who was the bookie. She ran all the numbers, collected and disbursed all the gambling money, and was feared more than anyone there. She was rumored to have ice flowing threw her veins. She never smiled except when she counted money. Her dress was always impeccable and so was her memory. She remembered every bet and the amount every person owed.

He also learned about a man who was the contact in the government. Which government, they didn't know. No one knew his name and when he came, he always wore a baseball cap or a cowboy hat that partially covered his face. People just called him "The Man." He was the man everyone in the area contacted to get the okay to have the fights. He was also the man everyone called if they needed the law off their butts.

As the people were taken into custody, more and more of the town had shown up. Marshall had kept one eye on Katelyn the whole time. He had just wanted one moment alone with her, but he knew his chances were slim when his sister had shown up along with Dani, Mo, and Ahmed. Then the rest of the town had shown up, and by the rest of the town, it was literally the rest of the town.

He just worried about her and couldn't wait to take her away from here. As the night went on, she looked more and more pale. She had taken a seat on the ground holding onto Ruffles the whole time. The humane society and some rescue groups had shown up a short time ago to help take the remaining dogs away to foster them and to hopefully rehabilitate them so they could be adopted. As the dogs were taken away and most of the criminals had either been transported to jail or the hospital, the crowd was starting to thin out. Maybe he could get some time with her before she went home. He had to tell her how much she meant to him and that he wanted her in his life, now and always.

He started to walk across the large clearing towards her when Alice's nose suddenly shot up. A breeze had rustled the leaves and brought with it the smell of an approaching summer storm. Alice stood up and pulled on her pink sequined leash.

"I think she needs to powder her nose. Can you take her Beauford?" Mrs. Wyatt asked as she handed her husband the leash.

"Of course, Sweet Pea. Come on Alice, there's my good girl."

Alice, with her nose to the wind, pulled Beauford across the clearing and around the ring to the far side of the area. There was a knocked over table that Alice began to sniff. The wind shifted and Alice followed it with her nose. She took deep sniffs of the air as she paced back and forth around the table alternating between smelling the air and sniffing the ground.

When the wind blew again, Alice's ears perked up and her nose shot up from the ground and towards the woods. She barked and rocketed into the woods, pulling the leash out of Beauford's hand as she ran under the crime scene tape and into the darkness surrounding the trees.

"Alice!" Beauford yelled as he followed her into the woods.

Marshall jogged across the clearing while the rest of the town went the long way, staying outside the crime scene tape to try to find Alice. He heard the twig snapping and the chatter of the town as they hurried to keep up with the Rose sisters leading the way. Off in the distance he heard Beauford calling for Alice and Alice barking. He ducked under the tape and looked into the darkness. He could see Beauford standing under a tree, trying to get the leash on Alice.

"What's going on Beauford?" Marshall called as he walked the twenty or so feet into the woods.

"I don't know. She just keeps running around this tree," Beauford called back.

"Beauford, dear, did you find her?" Mrs. Wyatt called out as she and the rest of the town approached through the woods.

"Yes, Sweet Pea, she's right here."

Alice jumped up with her front feet and clawed at the tree, barking. Marshall grabbed her collar and held her for Beauford, but Alice was refusing to be quiet. She lunged time and time again at the tree, looking up into the depth of the branches. Marshall looked up at the tree. There was something off, but he couldn't place it. Alice probably just treed a raccoon or possum.

"What's that up there?" Katelyn asked as she came to stand beside him.

"I don't know. My flashlight was dropped sometime while I was fighting."

"Here you go. I had mine in the truck," Cole said as he handed him a large mag light.

Everyone stepped closer as Marshall flashed the light up the tree. At first he didn't see anything, but then he saw a beige high heel hidden among the leaves. As the light traveled upward he followed the legs to the torn tight peach-colored skirt of the woman in the tree. Her face was hidden behind the trunk of the tree as she held on, trying to blend in.

"Is that a woman up there?" Miss Lily asked, squinting up the tree.

"Ma'am, this is the Keeneston Sheriff, you need to come down immediately." Marshall watched as the woman tried to disappear behind the tree trunk. "Ma'am, I need you to identify yourself immediately and come down from that tree." He pulled the gun Annie had given to him as he waited for her to acknowledge him.

"Are you stuck, dear?" Miss Violet called up, but then shrugged when the woman didn't answer.

The woman put one leg on the branch below and slowly climbed down a limb at a time. The only thing Marshall could tell about the woman was that her skirt was ripped up to her thigh as she climbed down the back of the tree.

She jumped the last couple of feet to the ground with her back to him. Her brown hair had started to fall out of its twist and leaves were stuck throughout it. She was average height, slim, and her suit said she had some money. She had a leather satchel over her shoulder that appeared to cost more than most people made in a month. This was not the type of person he expected to see hiding from the police.

"Okay, turn around slowly and keep your hands where we can see them," Marshall called out.

He felt, rather than saw Cole pull out his gun and aim it at the disheveled woman. Her back was stick straight as she slowly raised her hands. Beauford was holding onto Alice's leash with all his might as she growled at the woman. Katelyn was similarly struggling with Ruffles. Whoever this woman was, she was not liked.

The woman raised her hands to face level and slowly started to turn around. Gasps and whispers started on the far side of the town that saw her face first. Cole cocked his gun and Marshall did the same. Whoever it was, she was turning the town on its collective ear. As she turned to face him, he understood what had worked the town into a tizzy.

"Nancy?" he gasped.

He dropped his gun as she fully faced him. Her makeup was smeared and her normally perfect hair stuck out in various directions. Her white silk blouse was covered in dirt and her peach suit coat and skirt was ripped in many places. However, for all of her appearance, she held herself straight and with total confidence. She glared at the town and maintained the hoity air Marshall always hated.

"Would you care to explain what you were doing up a tree at an illegal dog fight?" Marshall asked.

"No, I wouldn't." She turned her nose to him and continued to stare at the town.

"The muffins," Marshall whispered.

"At your deputy's shooting?" Nuggett whispered back.

"Yes. She's known for her famous banana nut muffins. That's why it was bothering me. She had made me some just a couple of weeks ago." Turning to Nancy he raised his voice. "You shot Noodle, didn't you?"

The town gasped and Nancy just glared at them.

"You can't prove that."

"I can. Apparently shooting at an officer makes one hungry. You left behind a couple banana nut muffin wrappers."

Nancy didn't respond, but the town gasped collectively. It may not be enough evidence in a court, but it was the nail in the coffin according to the town. Everyone knew about Nancy's banana nut muffins.

"What are you all talking about? You're nothing but trash. You have no idea the work and information I have on people. But the worst of you all is you, you bitch." Nancy narrowed her eyes at Katelyn.

"If it weren't for you I'd have married Marshall and then known all about these plans. I could've kept the ring safe and secret and continued to make more money than you all could ever dream of. But, no, you have to come to town and distract him."

Marshall couldn't believe the venom she spewed. Her words were full of such hatred and elitism that he was temporarily stunned. The look on Katelyn's face changed from disbelief to horror as he realized he had lost his focus. Nancy had reached behind her back and pulled out a gun from under her suit jacket. She swung it toward Katelyn as Marshall raised his. Screams, barks, and gunshots filled the area.

Marshall froze as his eyes searched for Katelyn. He couldn't find her! He scanned the crowd again and found her lying on the ground, covered by Ruffles. His heart stopped as he feared the worse. Ruffles' tail thumped as Katelyn's arms came up from the ground and hugged her dog. She was alive!

He viewed the figure on the ground and knew Nancy was not so lucky. Looking around he saw Cole, Annie, Dinky, Nuggett, Romero, and Ahmed with their guns drawn.

"I told you I never liked her," Annie said dryly as she put away her gun.

"I've missed you Blake. Davies. Whatever. You're welcome back to the DEA anytime. I'll send you the ballistics on my gun for the investigation, Sheriff." Romero said as he went over to check Nancy's pulse, or lack thereof.

"Thank you. Now, stop trying to steal my deputy." Marshall bent down and picked up her satchel, even though every cell in his body was screaming to see Katelyn.

Inside he found a black, leather-bound book and approximately $100,000. He paused as he opened the book and stared at the names, the numbers, and the addresses of every gambler, dog fighter, and dealer that did business with her.

"Holy moly," Cole said with a whistle.

"My thoughts exactly."

"What's that?" Romero asked as he came up and looked over his shoulder. "Jesus H. Christ. We've been looking for some of these people and this is a whole book full."

"Us too. I'll call in the office. Operation Round Up starts in thirty minutes if Marshall will allow us access to that book." Cole said, looking at Marshall, raising his eyebrow in question.

"If we can meet at the FBI office in thirty, we can contact the agencies here and in Louisville, Nashville, and Knoxville. By morning we can round up everyone in this book." Romero had the look of a boy on Christmas morning as he stared at the names within the book.

"I'll put this into your custody as soon as Annie logs it into evidence. Get to it men." Marshall handed the book to Annie who slipped it into a clear evidence bag and started to label it.

He saw Katelyn stand up out of the corner of his eye. She was still surrounded by her grandparents, Paige, and the rest of the group of friends. She looked at him, and when her eyes met his he felt his heart break. She was so pale and she looked so lost and so tired. Marshall went to her then, no longer being able to stop the pull he felt when near her.

"Are you okay sweetheart?"

"Yes. Ruffles saved me, again. She jumped on me and pushed me to the ground," she said in awe.

"I think you have two dogs that need big treats when they get home," he bent down and gave each dog a hug as they wagged their tails. With all tension removed, they nudged each other playfully.

"That sounds like a wonderful idea. Let's get our girls home Sweet Pea." Beauford put his arm around Katelyn as Mrs. Wyatt took the dogs' leashes.

Now was not the time to tell her he loved her. He sighed and gave her a weak smile as she turned one last time to look at him before being put into Mrs. Wyatt's Lincoln, which Henry had just brought around for them.

"Mrs. Wyatt?" Marshall asked, his head tilted to the side as he looked at the car.

"Yes dear?"

"Is that barbed wire hanging off your car?"

"Yes, well, fencing was slowing us down so I just drove through it. I think it gives the car a certain look, don't you?"

Mrs. Wyatt got into the back seat with Katelyn as Ruffles leapt into the front passenger seat with Alice, vying for who got to stick their head out the window. Beauford drove off and Marshall couldn't help but smile as a ten-foot barbed wire tail followed behind.

He looked around, as the town was starting to break up and head home. No one noticed that his car had been parked a mile away or that he had driven up from the wrong direction. Or that he was in jeans when most everyone was used to seeing him in a suit or at least khakis.

The second he had seen Marshall storm into the clearing as a man possessed, he had known there was going to be a reckoning. He and Nancy had grabbed their things and had run. Although she had decided to hide up a tree, stupid girl. He had run into the woods and to his car. He was about to head home when his phone rang. It was his father telling him about the dog fight and informing him most of the town was already heading out there. Someone needed to represent the family, he had been told, and his father was in Frankfort and couldn't be there. Could he go for the family?

So, he had taken off his hat and mussed up his hair so it looked like he had just gotten out of bed. He pulled out the set of dentures and tossed them in the glove box along with the colored contacts, fake eyebrows and mustache. Then he had sat there and worried about Nancy. He knew his name wasn't in that black book of hers, as she never wrote down his bets. However, she was the one person who knew his real identity. If she talked, he'd be arrested in a heartbeat.

After half the town had driven by his hiding spot, he turned on the car and drove out of the woods and parked behind a minivan. He had hurried to the scene and put himself right in the middle of the crowd and demanded to know what happened. He had scanned the crowd and the grounds for Nancy and thought he was home free until that stupid mutt found her up the tree.

He was sure she'd give him up. He let others push past him to see what was going on as Nancy climbed down the tree. He was at the back of the crowd when she turned around. But, the dumb bitch lost her temper over that vet. She had complained to him about Katelyn for months and he guessed she just lost it seeing her there now. She had laughed and laughed when Andre showed up with Ruffles. He had never seen her so excited as she was to see Katelyn watch her dog get torn to shreds.

When Nancy saw Katelyn holding her dog, still alive and well, it must have triggered something in her. She had pulled out that gun and pointed it at Katelyn and then the answer to his dilemma presented itself. He had hidden his smile under his hand as Nancy was shot dead by half the people there!

He could now go forward with the merger into Internationals as planned. Upper management had already tapped him to be their ears in Washington and to quietly lobby for the protection of dog fighters. He had done such a good job keeping the law away from the fights in Kentucky over the past five years that he hoped they were willing to overlook this downfall. In fact, he would make sure they blamed it on the Watkinses.

On top of that, he had quietly lobbied for reduced sentencing for people convicted of crimes related to dog-fighting and had managed to stop many bills from even coming up for a vote in Keeneston and in Frankfort. He may not have been a regular member on Kentucky's Capitol Hill, but he had the connections that Internationals liked. Internationals had contacted him about his connections in Washington and he couldn't be more excited. With the money from Internationals backing his bid for office, he would be elected in no time. Senator did have a nice ring to it, didn't it?

"Good night, Sheriff. Good work here tonight."

"Thank you," Marshall said to him.

"Let me know if there's anything I or my family can help you with."

"Yes, I will. Good night."

He turned and headed towards his car with a smile hidden under the stern expression he wore on his face.

"Ah, ladies, may I escort you to your car? I'd hate to have you trip on a root or anything."

"Thank you. How kind of you." Miss Violet said as she took his outstretched arm.

He felt like whistling. No one suspected a thing and they never would.

Chapter Twenty

Marshall straightened up his back and stretched. It was quiet now as he sat in the cruiser and took notes of the scene. Everyone was gone. All the evidence was collected and logged. All the criminals were in jail or the hospital. He had fielded questions from the press and was now working on his report and his personal notes. He knew he'd need them for the countless trials coming up.

Cole had checked in with him and told him the book contained thousands of names all over the Southeast. They were working with numerous government agencies in fifteen different states. At eight in the morning, just two hours from now, doors were going to be busted in all over the south as the people in the black book were rounded up.

Headlights made their way down the dirt road and he pushed himself out of his seat to see who it was. He recognized his brother's car instantly and leaned against the cruiser and waited for him to stop his car.

"Heard you had a long night."

"The king of understatement. It looks like you had a long night too, Mi."

His brother looked exhausted. There were bags under his eyes. Miles' hair looked like it had been run over and over by his hand.

"Work has been crazy to say the least. I'm just trying to figure some corporate stuff out."

"Anything I can help with?" Marshall asked, knowing Miles would never ask for help.

"Not yet. How's Katelyn?"

"I don't know," he sighed. "I can't get a minute alone with her. I've been trying to tell her I love her for days, but something always happens or someone always walks in." He was beyond frustrated now.

"It'll work out. Is there anything you need my help with?"

"No, I don't think so. I was actually just about to head home," Marshall told his brother.

"Good. Then follow me to the road. I'll see you tonight at Ma's for dinner. Oh, and put some ice on that eye before Ma sees you."

"Good idea. I hate when she fusses. 'Night Miles."

Katelyn stared at her ceiling and tried to imagine sheep jumping over the bed. It didn't work and it hadn't worked for the past three hours since her grandparents had ushered her into bed.

She really just wanted to know how Marshall was. His eye had already turned black and blue. There was a cut across his chin that he really should have been stitched, but he had just had a paramedic put some butterfly strips on it and said Cade could stitch it up later.

But, her grandparents never gave her the option to check on him. She had been so scared and she really wanted Marshall's arms wrapped around her and to feel the strength of his chest as she leaned into him. Instead she was stuck surrounded by the town, staring longingly at him as if he was an oasis just out of reach. She watched him work as she clung to Ruffles. He commanded the area. He answered questions and gave orders with such a calm confidence. When Nancy had raised that gun at her the only thought that ran through her mind was of him. She had waited too long. She should've taken a chance.

Katelyn really wanted to see him. She sat up slowly in bed, feeling foolish for this urgency that had come over her. Swinging her feet onto the rug, Katelyn stood up. Pain shot through her side where she had been hit in her wound during the incident. She knew she had torn a stitch or two during her struggle with her captors too.

Katelyn stood up and made her way to the full-length antique mirror that stood in the corner of her room. She pulled up her white tank top and stared at the reflection in the mirror. Marshall wasn't the only one who was black and blue. One side of her ribcage was nothing but a big bruise. She certainly wouldn't be running anywhere, even into his arms.

She lowered her shirt and went to look out into the morning light when a soft knock at the door stopped her.

"Come in."

Katelyn turned around and watched her door open. Her heartbeat sped up and she had butterflies in her stomach. Had Marshall come for her?

"Dad? What are you doing here?"

"Your grandmother called and I jumped on the jet as soon as I could. I'm sorry it took me so long to get here. I was in LA checking on some of my properties when I got the call. She said you were hurt. You look horrible."

Jack Jacks stood in all his corporate glory and, for once in his life, looked worried.

"Thanks a lot for the lovely compliment. I'm okay, Dad."

"No, no you're not." He strode forward and before she knew what he was doing he pulled up the side of her shirt, exposing the long, angry gash on her side. "What's that long incision and how did you get covered in bruises?"

"It's a gunshot wound. And the bruises are from my abduction last night."

"Shot? My daughter has been shot and kidnapped? Samuel, get in here!" He yelled into the hall.

Katelyn watched as a young man in skinny jeans, black-rimmed glasses, and a button-down shirt straight off the Calvin Klein runway popped into the room. His hair was gelled so it was hard to tell if it was brown or if it was just wet.

"Yes Mr. Jacks?"

"I need you to find the leading expert on gunshot wounds and the best plastic surgeon in the world and fly them here immediately."

"Stop. Dad, I'm fine. It's just a bruise and the wound is healing well. Don't fly in any doctors. I'll just refuse to see them."

Her father stepped forward and placed a kiss on her forehead. "If you say so. Will you at least get back into bed and rest?"

"That's right, dear, you need your rest for dinner tonight at the Davies farm," her grandmother said as she peeked around Samuel in the doorway.

"Why would she care about a dinner at a farm? No, she's going to stay in bed and I am going to fly my personal chef in to make you dinner. You're too good and important for dinner at a *farm*."

"Jack! That is it! I've put up with your snobbery long enough. I put up with it first because you were married to my daughter. Then I put up with it because of Katelyn. But, if you say one more narrow-minded, pompous word… bless your heart, I will shoot you. Gosh knows I've had practice lately," her grandmother said in a raised voice.

Katelyn snorted and then laughed out loud at her father's shocked expression and that this was the angriest she'd ever heard her grandmother. It was hard to take her too seriously as she stood with her hands on her hips and a huge yellow hat with a white feather on her head that bounced as she lectured in her slow sing-song voice.

"Look Ruth, I don't expect you to know the finer points of life…" her father started to say.

"Alice, petunia!"

Katelyn heard Alice's nails click on the hardwood floor as she ran down the hall and into her bedroom. She looked to see where her grandmother was pointing and then sprung up and took a bite out of the seat of her father's thousand dollar pants.

"Petunia? Your dog bit my ass!"

"Well, any proper southern lady would never use such vulgar language. As for the finer points in life, you wouldn't know them if they jumped up and bit you in the petunia."

"And you would? Sure, you have a little money from investments, but that's it. I have hundreds of millions and I'm surrounded by only the best clothes, food, planes, cars, houses, and people, while you're out to dinner with farmers!" Her father laughed then and by the pinched face her grandmother was giving him, Katelyn bet he was about to be given a lesson.

"You want to know the finer points of life? Then I'll give you a lesson young man. You're talking to a direct daughter of one of the founding members of the Daughters of the American Revolution. My family tree, when shaken, has so many debutants falling out of it that you'd be lost in a cloud of white tulle. And, don't forget, while your grandfather, the Scottish *farmer*, got off the boat, my father had, and I still have, a house next to the old Vanderbilt compound in the Hamptons. Further, I doubt you have millions of dollars in family silver buried in the back yard from the Civil War, either. See, the only people who point out the finer points of life, while looking down their nose at others, are the ones who are too new to money to know better than to behave so poorly!"

"But, Sylvia never said anything about the Hamptons, or silver in the backyard, or anything at all about money. Besides wanting mine."

"That's because we cut her off after she trashed the house in the Hamptons during a massive fight with husband number two. Now, enough of this money talk, and enough of your snobbery. I hope you've learned that you never know what fortune, money or otherwise, can be found with good manners and learning what's beneath the surface of a person."

"Yes, Mrs. Wyatt. I believe I understand." Her father hung his head and Katelyn was left shocked as her grandmother smacked her father's arm.

"Bless your heart, you can still call me Mom." She wrapped her arms around his neck and pulled him in for a kiss on the forehead.

Her father smiled and looked at her as if it was the first time. Katelyn smiled back—she'd see what changes really came about, but right now she was having a hard time not laughing about the image of her father with a bright red lipstick mark right in the middle of his forehead.

"So, who are these people we're having dinner with tonight?" he asked.

"Your daughter's beau."

"A farmer? My daughter is dating a farmer?" he choked.

"Would that be so bad as long as she's happy? Now, I'm off to call Marcy to see if you can even come to dinner. After all, you haven't been invited." Her grandmother gave him a wicked little grin and floated off down the hall with Alice trailing behind her, a piece of black suit hanging from her lips.

"Does he make you happy?" her father asked quietly.

"Yes, he does."

Katelyn felt the warming sense of love take over her body and heart. She couldn't wait to see Marshall. She wanted to see him with her grandmother and grandfather and to feel that joyful peace of being in love and being happy.

"Well, I guess I can put up with having a farmer in the family then. Luckily I have enough time to find a new pair of pants and then I'll come back and check on you. Maybe we could spend the afternoon together?"

"I'd like that." She even meant it this time.

Katelyn couldn't stop wringing her hands. She should've driven. Instead she was in the back seat of her grandfather's Cadillac, next to her father who was wrapping up a phone call. Finally they arrived at the large farmhouse. She jumped out of the car and hurried around the car as the rest of her family got out.

"So, it really is a farm. How quaint," her father said as he buttoned his suit jacket.

She looked down at her jeans and colorful wrap shirt she picked up on a photo shoot in Greece. Maybe she should've worn a skirt? She looked up at the house when she heard laughter and raised voices floating out into the night. She had been so eager to get here, but now she was afraid to go in. What would happen if his family didn't like her? Of course she and Paige had been friends for a while, but dating her brother was something different.

"You coming, dear, or are you going to just stand here and stare?" her grandmother asked as she walked up the stairs and rang the bell.

"Come on, I want to meet this boyfriend of yours." Her father held out his arm and she gladly took it as they made their way into the house.

Katelyn stepped through the threshold and scanned the room looking for Marshall. She saw Marcy giving her grandmother a kiss, Jake was talking to Miles, Pierce and Cade were teasing Cole, and Paige and Annie looked like they were comparing their slightly rounded tummies.

"Which one's yours? I like the one in the suit."

"That's Miles, he's the oldest. He's in corporate agriculture. I don't see Marshall yet. Come on, I'll introduce you to everyone." Katelyn began to lead her father over to Miles when Marcy intercepted them.

"Oh, Mr. Jacks, it is so wonderful to have you in our home. I sure hope you're hungry. We've got fried chicken, fresh sweet potatoes, and sweet corn that we just picked. Then I made a huge chocolate trifle with bourbon caramel for dessert. Let me introduce you to my husband."

Marcy grabbed his arm and steered him through the crowd over to her husband while talking to him about all her kids. Katelyn figured her father was in good hands and headed over where Paige and Annie were waving at her.

"Have you been filled in on the investigation?" Paige asked.

"No, what happened after I left?"

"Cole called in the full force of the FBI..."

"And Romero, my old boss, called in the DEA..." Annie put in for Paige.

"They all met up at Cole's office and went through the book they got off of Nancy. It had names of all the drug dealers, the gunrunners, and the people participating in the dog-fighting ring. Well, you know how well she managed the Belle's annual fundraiser, it was no wonder she kept such particular notes. Anyway," Paige continued, "It took over one hundred officers from state and federal law enforcement agencies, but by this morning close to three hundred people had been charged."

"Of course, some were charged on small things like illegal gambling. But, some were charged with serious drug and weapons charges. They even found a man who was involved in human trafficking that they had been looking for," Annie told her.

Katelyn hugged herself with her arms. She was happy so many people were going to be brought to justice, but she still saw the crazy look in the dog's eyes when he lunged to attack her and Ruffles. It was the same look Nancy had when she pointed the gun at her. She feared she'd dream of those moments for the rest of her life.

She glanced back around the room and saw that Cade was now talking to her grandfather and by the gestures she bet it was about football. Marcy had taken her grandmother to the kitchen. Miles and her father looked to be in a serious corporate discussion.

"Katelyn," Jake touched her elbow to draw her attention.

"Oh, hello Mr. Davies. Thank you for inviting us for dinner. After all the events recently, it'll be nice to have a big dinner like this."

She looked up at Mr. Davies in his Kentucky Athletics t-shirt. His brown hair was starting to turn gray, but his body showed years of working outside. His arms were large and muscular and his skin was deeply tanned.

"You're welcome anytime. You're good for him, you know?"

"I'm sorry?" What was he talking about?

"You keep Marshall on his toes, just like my sweet Marcy does. And call me Jake." With a wink he headed to the other side of the room to talk to Pierce.

The front door opened and Katelyn watched as Marshall strode in. He looked tired, but so very handsome. He wore jeans that sat low on his waist with a worn brown leather belt. His eye was swollen and matched his dark blue shirt. She smiled nervously and was about to head over to him when Paige stopped her.

"What do you think of Bridget for a girl's name?"

"Hmm? I'm sorry, what did you ask?" Katelyn tried to focus on Paige, but she kept watching Marshall as Cole walked over to him.

Marshall was sure he was part of the walking dead now. He was so tired he could barely stand. By the time he wrapped up the paperwork, did press interviews over the phone, and visited the jail to interrogate witnesses, it was almost time for dinner. He had wanted to go see Katelyn, but his mother had called twice, once interrupting a video interview with Anderson Cooper, to make sure he came to the weekly family dinner.

So, instead of going to see Katelyn, he had run home and showered before heading over to his parents' house. When he pulled up to the house he became worried when he saw the car parked by the front door. That area was reserved for guests and he didn't recognize the car. He was quite fearful of a set up. Some woman his mom met at the grocery store, or some nurse's daughter, or just some girl she saw in the mall. His mother was very friendly, much to his displeasure.

Being the coward he was when it came to his mother, he had tried to sneak in the door and without being noticed, but Cole had spotted him immediately. He kept his head down and tried to hide himself behind Cole as they talked. He just wasn't in the mood for some ditzy blonde his mom found. There was only one blonde he wanted.

"Saw you on the news," Cole said with a grin.

"Which one?"

"All of them. Thanks for crediting the FBI and DEA for the roundup today. I know both my boss and Romero's were very happy with the praise you gave us. I even got a call from the Director congratulating me on the bust and complimenting us for our inter-agency work."

"You guys deserve it. That roundup was orchestrated to perfection."

"Thanks. Oh, it looks like I need to go see my wife and let you have a chat with your potential father-in-law," Cole winked and then laughed at the confused look on Marshall's face.

"So, you're the farmer my daughter is dating."

Marshall turned around and came face to face with Jack Jacks. That had to mean Katelyn was here. He scanned the room and found her surrounded by Paige, Annie, Cade, and Cole.

"I'm sorry, farmer?" Didn't Mr. Jacks recognize him? And why did he think Katelyn was dating a farmer?

"Yes, my daughter's dating a farmer and he wasn't here yet. Since you just got here, I'm guessing you're the farmer."

"I'm not a farmer."

"Oh, then I guess you're not him."

"I'm pretty sure I'm him."

"But you said you're not a farmer."

"I'm not. I'm the Sheriff of Keeneston."

"Oh, I know you. You wouldn't arrest those old ladies. I guess you were right about that now that I think about it. Just didn't recognize you out of uniform. So, who is this farmer my daughter is dating?"

Marshall took a deep breath and let it out slowly. What was this about a farmer? Did he think because he owned a farm he was just a farmer? He guessed technically he was a farmer. Ah crap, now he was all confused about it.

"Excuse me, sir, I think I'll ask Katelyn about that myself."

Marshall took a step towards Katelyn. She looked up and saw him then. They both smiled and he lengthened his stride to reach her side quicker.

"Hey, I need to talk to you."

"What is it Miles? Now's not the best time."

"Morgan's back in town."

"Morgan? Not *the* Morgan?" Holy cow. How many more surprises could he get today?

"Oh, good! You're here. We can sit down for dinner now." Marcy sang out to the crowd the second she saw him.

"We'll talk later?" Miles asked.

"Definitely."

His brothers pushed him toward his seat in the dining room and his mother took Katelyn's hand and led her right past him to her seat directly across from his at the long table. Marshall sat down and almost groaned when Mr. Jacks sat down next to him. Beauford took the other seat next to him and immediately started talking crops with his father.

"I guess he didn't show up," Mr. Jacks said he sat down next to Marshall. "I was really hoping to meet this guy."

"I think there's been some miscommunication here. I'm pretty sure the man you want to meet is me."

"You? Are you dating my daughter too?"

"No, I mean yes. I am dating your daughter, and to my knowledge, I'm the *only* man dating your daughter."

"So you're a farmer and a sheriff?" Marshall paused and then nodded. Technically he was correct. "Well, if you're the one dating my little girl, I have some questions for you."

Damn. Maybe he shouldn't have said anything after all. He looked across the table at Katelyn who was sandwiched between Miles and Pierce. If he thought he had it bad, she had it worst.

He leaned forward across his plate and whispered, "Psst. Katelyn."

"Didn't anyone tell you it was rude to whisper at the table?"

"Shut up Pierce."

He leaned forward again, "Katelyn, I need to talk to you after dinner."

"What?" she whispered back.

Marshall put his elbows on the table and leaned forward again, "I said…"

"What's the matter, son? Why can't you sit still? You got ants in your pants?" Beauford laughed.

"I was going to ask the same thing," Mr. Jacks mumbled as he took another bite of his fried chicken.

"I was just trying to talk to Katelyn." Marshall let out a sigh and sat back in his chair. It was hopeless.

"Well go ahead, she's right there." Mr. Jacks pointed at Katelyn who flushed red as Miles and Pierce turned to look at her.

"No one is stopping you, son. Go ahead and talk." Beauford slapped him on the back.

"At least he wants to talk to her with his clothes on this time," Mrs. Wyatt said from the other end of the table. "This chicken is wonderful Marcy!"

His mother sputtered, Pierce laughed so hard he was worried he'd fall out of his chair, Mr. Jacks became very still next to him, and Katelyn was red as a beet. Then suddenly everyone started talking at once. He heard Mrs. Wyatt telling the story of walking in on him, not just once, but three times while he was naked in her house. Beauford was having fun talking about pointing a gun at him. Pierce was being Pierce, his sister was giggling, and Miles was even laughing. He couldn't take it anymore! He slammed his hand down on the table as he stood up so fast it sent his chair falling to the ground.

"Dammit! I am trying to tell her I love her!"

Silence met his ears as everyone turned and stared at him. Beauford cleared his throat and slowly put down his fork and knife.

"Son, did you forget my advice on wooing her?"

"I love you too!" Katelyn blurted out. She sat back in her chair and smiled at him. "I love you too, Marshall!" she said slower and quieter this time.

His heart soared and he wanted to leap across the table and pull her into his arms. She was his, all his, and he couldn't wait to show her how much she meant to him.

"Well, I believe it's time for dessert. Everyone into the living room!" Marcy stood and ushered everyone out of the dining room.

"You want to get out of here?" Marshall asked from across the table once Pierce was finally dragged away by his mother.

"Yes!"

Marshall ran around the table and scooped her up into his arms. He kissed her then like a man possessed with love. She writhed against him as he feasted on her mouth. His tongue tasted hers as he deepened the kiss even more. He felt, rather than heard, her moan as she flung herself into the kiss. He felt her fingers clutching the back of his head, urging him on.

"Come on. We'll go out the back," he grinned as he reluctantly pulled away and put her small hand into his.

He had never felt so alive or so invincible in his life. If she was by his side he could do anything.

Chapter Twenty-One

Marshall opened his door and led Katelyn into the living room. Bob strode out of the kitchen with spaghetti sauce all over his face. It looked like he learned how to open the refrigerator door. It was only a matter of time.

He turned to Katelyn and realized she was suddenly shy. He pulled her into his arms and she laid her head on his shoulder. It fit perfectly. He placed a gentle kiss on her neck and when she leaned further into him he moved his lips up her neck. She shivered as he made his way across her jaw and then seized her lips with his. After he had his feast, he pulled back and ran his hands through her hair.

"How can you possibly love me when I've been such an ass to you?"

"You're just too loveable to resist once I saw under the hard exterior you put on." She paused and then looked him in the eyes, "I also understand why you thought I was cold. I had to finally trust someone. And even when you were being an ass, you were always looking out for me. I could always trust you to be there for me. When I looked into my heart, I found you had already taken up residence there."

"Is there room for me to take permanent residency in your heart?" He whispered.

"I think you already have."

"Katelyn Jacks, will you let me love you and stand proudly by your side for the rest of our lives as your husband?" He took her hands in his and went down on one knee, "Will you marry me?"

"Yes!"

Marshall's heart filled with joy as he picked her up and twirled her around. Her head was flung backward as she laughed out loud with happiness. He slid her body down his and pulled her face to his. He kissed her then, his fiancé, his love.

She ran her hands down his back and he felt like roaring when she squeezed his bottom and pulled his shirt from his jeans. He raised his arms and let her peel it off and fling it to the ground. He was already working the buttons on the side of her shirt. When he got them undone, he unwrapped her, exposing her to him as the material parted and fell to the ground.

"Wait!" she gasped.

"What's the matter?"

"Is the door locked?" she asked and then they laughed.

He scooped her up into his arms and kissed her. He carried her towards the front of the house and locked the door before heading up the stairs.

"This time no one is going to interrupt us."

Katelyn squeezed her eyes shut and buried her head into the pillow. Her eyes were scratchy and heavy with tiredness. Her body throbbed as she stretched out in bed. Slowly she opened her eyes halfway and took in the sight of Marshall lying next to her in bed. She ran her eyes down his naked chest and over his...

"Good morning sweetheart." His voice rumbled over her and her body instantly responded.

"Good morning."

"How do you feel?" He ran his hand down her side and stopped on the curve of her bare hip.

"Excellent. However, I do think we'll need to sleep at some point."

"Not anytime soon," he said as his hand disappeared under the sheet.

Katelyn closed the kennel door and wrote down her directions for Bekah. She yawned and then stretched, still feeling the effects of their lovemaking from this morning. They had grudgingly gotten out of bed and headed to work after his phone rang for the fifth time.

Work had seemed like a blur and all she could think about was the dinner plans they had for tonight. Just two more clients to go and then she could head home, take a shower, and change before going to Marshall's house.

She walked into the exam room and smiled. She was vaccinating a litter of puppies for the K-9 training facility in Lexington. She gave large discounts to dogs being trained for service, and as a result was the vet for many of the surrounding counties' police dogs and search and rescue dogs. Katelyn played with the litter of seven German Shepherd puppies and knew this was just one of the reasons she loved her job.

After vaccinating the puppies, she saw a client with Mr. Purrfect, a very large black cat with a white spot that resembled a bowtie at his neck. She said goodbye to her last client and to Mr. Purrfect and hurried to enter all the information into the computer.

"Am I interrupting?" the accent-laden voice said.

"Ahmed! Of course not. I wanted to thank you for the other night. I know you were one of the people who stopped Nancy from killing me."

"I will always be here if you need me."

"I know you will. Thank you."

"I hear congratulations are in order." He smiled and she felt the familiar friendship again.

"Yes. I still can't believe it."

"I can. I've never seen a man so in love. I do hope I am invited to the wedding."

"You know you are."

Ahmed took her hand and placed a small kiss on her knuckles, "Blessings to you and Marshall," he said before leaving.

Katelyn went back to work and the thought of having a Man of Honor crossed her mind. It might be fun to tell Ahmed he had to wear a dress.

"This is a nice place you have here."

"Dad?"

"I wanted to stop by and see this place you've put together. It's state of the art, I couldn't be prouder."

"Thanks, Dad." Her father gave her a hug and she tried to remember the last time he had done that.

"I heard about the wedding, congratulations."

"Ah, the Keeneston Grapevine."

"No, your young man stopped by and saw me this morning. He didn't ask permission to marry you, but he did assure me he loved you and would take excellent care of you. I hope you two will be very happy. I must say — I like him a lot. Do you think I could get his mother to become our head cook at the hotel in Nashville?"

"I don't think so," she laughed.

"Too bad. I hope you don't mind if I hang around a little while. I would really like to get to know you and Marshall. I have a feeling I'll like him quite a bit. I respect men who stand up to me, something he's already done."

"I'd really like that."

"As a wedding gift, why don't you pick whatever hotel you want in the world for your wedding. I'll even fly everyone out myself."

"Thanks Dad." She was touched by his gesture and knew he was trying to mend fences. "But, I think I really want the wedding at Wyatt Estate." That was home for her and it would mean more to her than anything to get married there.

"Dad, I do have a favor to ask you. I want you and grandpa to walk me down the aisle." She watched as her dad's eyes got misty and he nodded.

"I'd be honored to."

Marshall bounded up the stairs to the clinic and went inside. He said hi to Shelly and loved hearing her congratulate him on getting engaged. Just thinking about marrying Katelyn made him happier than he had ever been.

"Hey sweetheart. Oh, hello Mr. Jacks." Marshall held out his hand and shook his soon to be father-in-law's hand.

"You can call me Jay. That's what only my closest friends call me. I'll let you two go, but I wanted to see if you all would join me for dinner tomorrow night."

"Sure. That works for me, what about your schedule sweetheart?" he asked Katelyn who had a happy, dopey look on her face.

"Perfect."

They said good-bye to Jay and he pulled her into a kiss.

"I've wanted to do that all day. I missed you."

"Same here." She tilted her head up and kissed him gently before laying her head on his chest.

"I have a surprise for you."

"I love surprises." She stepped back from him and clapped her hands.

He handed her a large-sized box wrapped in beautiful white paper with a blue ribbon. He could hardly keep his hands off of her as she ripped the paper off and opened the box. She laughed and held up the two shiny new deadbolts.

"This is the best gift you could have given me." she laughed.

"Did you see the key?"

She picked up the key ring with two keys and a large diamond ring on it and gasped. He took it from her hand and unhooked the engagement ring. It was a solitaire diamond framed by two

...ires that reminded him of the color of her eyes when she was
...ing love to him.

He took her hand in his and slid the ring onto her finger. He met
...atelyn's eyes and felt as if his life was just beginning.

"I love you, Katelyn. For now and always. I look forward to
everyday and every new adventure we will share together."

"I love you too. Now, how are you going to tell Bob he's getting a
sister?"

"Let's go home, my beautiful fiancé, and introduce our kids."

"Yes, let's go home." She smiled when he slung his arm around
her shoulders and kissed the top of her head. She had just found her
happily ever after and she intended to cherish every moment.

Epilogue

H e stepped off the plane at the Ronald Reagan International Airport and surveyed his new domain. Washington D.C. had him truly excited. He had received a phone call from the head of Internationals asking him to come for a face-to-face.

He made his way through the terminal and headed outside to the packed sidewalk. He pushed his way past a family and held out his hand to hail a cab. Maybe he'd have him drive to the Capitol so he could get a glimpse of where his new office would be come election time. He glanced down at his watch and saw he didn't have enough time. He needed to get across the Potomac and over to a warehouse in the southeast part of the city first, then he'd take a tour of the Capitol after his meeting.

He gave the cab driver the address and sat back to enjoy the trip. He'd been here with his father, of course, for numerous political conferences. His father was always away in Washington serving as an advisor for agriculture to many of the congressmen from the South. His father was always so close to the power, but never held it. Now he would do what his father never did. Become a senator.

The cab slowed at an old warehouse close to the river and let him out. The driver sped away quickly leaving him standing alone. Not afraid of his surroundings, he looked around the area with a business eye. It was isolated from the main streets. The surrounding buildings seemed abandoned and in a state of decay, but the one he was instructed to go to was in pretty good shape. It would do nicely for fighting. The area afforded many ways in and out. He doubted any neighbors would complain about the noise.

Within minutes of the cab's departure, a shiny black stretch limo drove in from the south side. He smiled as he watched it slow to a stop near him. He would have a limo like that one day. The far door opened and a large man in a black suit and a deep red shirt opened at the neck stepped out. He was easily six feet and his shaved head gleamed in the sunlight. His muscles fought against the constraint of his suit jacket as he closed the door. He watched the man, obviously a bodyguard, walk around the back of the car and stand next to the door. The window slowly lowered and the profile of a man appeared.

"Sir, I just want to say I am honored to represent you and our causes in Washington." He stood straight and waited for his praise.

"It seems, Mr. Russell, that you have failed me."

Paul Russell stood speechless. Failed? He hadn't failed! He'd run the most profitable dog fighting ring in the South.

"You failed when you allowed a backwoods sheriff to come in and take down hundreds of my men. You cost me hundreds of thousands of dollars in loss of trade through the weapons and drug deals. You allowed them to be arrested, to be interrogated, and you allowed them to find that damn bitch and her book."

"I couldn't help that," Paul whined. Damn that Nancy! That bitch was screwing him constantly, even from her grave.

"Yes you could have. You could have shot her and taken the book in the confusion. More importantly, if you had been doing your job this raid would have never happened in the first place."

Paul couldn't help the tremor that ran through his body at the deadly quiet tone of the man in car. He looked around at his surroundings again and suddenly didn't feel quite as secure. He realized just how isolated they were and the fact that he had nowhere to run even if he dared to try. He also realized no one knew where he was or would hear him if he screamed.

"I'll make it up to you. When I am in the Senate, I will do anything you want," he pleaded.

"Enough. I don't bargain and I don't listen to begging." The man snapped. "Sergei," he said with a nod as he started to roll up the tinted window.

Paul felt his heart speed up as Sergei took a step towards him. He turned to run, but the warehouses closed in on him. He didn't know where to go, where to turn. He heard the sound of metal scraping and turned to see Sergei pulling a wicked looking sword from a scabbard hidden beneath his suit jacket.

"Please, please, you don't have to do this," he begged as he darted around the circular area outlined by the warehouses.

Paul held up his hands as he felt his back press up against one of the decaying buildings. His eyes widened as Sergei raised his arm across his chest, the sunlight danced across the blade in his hand the second before it came swiping down.

He put his hand to his neck and felt the warmth of his blood flowing over his fingers. Paul's knees buckled and he fell to the ground. He lay, fatally wounded, waiting for death to come. This time, there was no applause or profit to be had.

About the Author

Kathleen Brooks is the bestselling author of the Bluegrass Series. She has garnered attention as a new voice in romance with a warm Southern feel. Her books feature quirky small town characters you'll feel like you've known forever, romance, humor, and mystery all mixed into one perfect glass of sweet tea.

Kathleen is an animal lover who supports rescue organizations and other non-profit organizations whose goals are to protect and save our four-legged family members.

Kathleen lives in Central Kentucky with her husband, daughter, two dogs, and a cat who thinks he's a dog. She loves to hear from readers and can be reached at Kathleen@Kathleen-Brooks.com

Check out the Website (www.kathleen-brooks.com) for updates on the Bluegrass Series. You can also "Like" Kathleen on Facebook (www.facebook.com/pages/Lexington-KY/Kathleen-Brooks/143823225691578) and follow her on Twitter @BluegrassBrooks.

Bluegrass Brothers Series Continues!

Love Keeneston? Don't want to say good-bye? Then don't! The next book in the Bluegrass Brothers Series will be Mile's story. Is Keeneston ready for the return of one of its most notorious bad girls? Will straight-laced Miles play by the rules, or will he find the reward to be worth the risk?

So, make a pitcher of special iced tea, cut a slice of pecan pie, and get ready for some more Southern charm from your favorite town!

Want to know when the next book is published? Go sign up on the contact form on kathleen-brooks.com. I will email you as soon as the next book is published.

Made in the USA
Lexington, KY
31 July 2018